Stilettos & Stetsons

A WEBSITE ROMANCE

First Edition

ISBN 979-8-9912539-4-9

Cover Design by Lou Designs

A WEBSITE ROMANCE

SUZIE TERRY

Contents

To my beloved husband,

Through every challenge and triumph, you have been my steadfast partner. Your rugged strength and tender heart mirror the essence of Rex, while our adventures remind me of Sophia's courage to embrace new beginnings. Our love story, like theirs, is filled with passion, renewal, and the promise of tomorrow.

Thank you for being my rock, my confidant, and my greatest love. This book is a celebration of the enduring power of love, a testament to our shared journey, and a reflection of the beautiful life we continue to build together.

With all my heart,
Suzie

CHAPTER 1
Profiles And Pings

Sophia Sanders stood on the veranda of her condo, the soft breeze carrying the scent of salt and sun-bleached sand. Below her, the bay of Cabo San Lucas sparkled like liquid sapphire under the afternoon sun, the iconic arches framing the horizon in a timeless dance between land and sea. This view had become her daily ritual, a quiet moment to watch the world drift by on the turquoise waves, cruise ships slowly making their way into the bay, as they had done countless times before.

She took a deep breath, the warmth of the sun kissing her skin, and closed her eyes. It was hard to believe how much her life had changed in such a short time. Not long ago, she and Keith had stood here together, their hearts full of plans and dreams for a peaceful retirement in this paradise. They had built this home together, every detail carefully chosen for the life they would share. But life, with its unpredictable currents, had other plans.

Keith's illness had come swiftly, like a storm out of a clear sky. Idiopathic Pulmonary Fibrosis, the doctors had said. A terminal condition, no cure, only time left to manage the inevitable. Sophia had barely had time to process the diagnosis before she found herself back in the United States, the unfamiliar cold of the hospital room in sharp contrast to the warmth of Cabo. She had been strong for him, navigating the unfamiliar world of hospice care, fighting back her own grief as she watched Keith's life slip away.

When Keith finally passed, Sophia had returned to Cabo, alone. His ashes rested now beneath the waves, set free from a yacht surrounded by friends who had come to honor his memory. The sea had taken him in, a final resting place in the waters they had both loved.

Now, it was just her and the sea, the only constants in a world that had been turned upside down. She wasn't sure what her future held, but one thing was certain: Cabo was her home, and it was here that she would find a way to rebuild her life, one piece at a time.

Sophia reclined in a plush lounge chair, the vibrant colors of her sundress contrasting against the cool, neutral tones of her spacious living room. The scent of saltwater drifted in through the partially open sliding windows, mingling with the faint aroma of fresh coffee. A gentle breeze teased the pages of the book she held in her hands, shielding her face from the midday sun. Her lips curled into a soft, almost absent-minded smile as she occasionally flicked her gaze toward the iPhone resting on a nearby stool, its screen dark and waiting.

For a while, Sophia remained in that pose, her fingers gripping the well-worn edges of *The Perks of Being a Wallflower.* But after a few moments, she sighed, a deep, heavy breath that seemed to carry the weight of unsaid thoughts. She sat up, her green eyes—once bright with the vitality of youth but now softened by time and experience—flickered toward her phone. No new notifications. She shifted her hold on the book, now holding it with one hand, while her other hand absentmindedly rubbed her brows, as if trying to massage them.

The morning was slipping away, the clock on the wall nudging closer to noon. Sophia's gaze lingered on it, her mind wandering far from the words on the page. Memories and plans, joys and regrets—all of it seemed to swirl together in the quiet of her mind. The large living room, with its minimalist decor and panoramic views of the ocean, felt unusually empty.

She turned her attention back to the expansive sliding windows. The scene outside was idyllic: serene waters stretching out to meet the horizon, cruise ships anchored in the bay, and the iconic arches of Cabo framing the picturesque view. It was a sight she had grown accustomed to, yet it never failed to captivate her. But today, even the ocean's calm beauty couldn't fully hold her attention

Sophia returned to her book, trying to recapture the initial grip the story had on her. But as she attempted to lose herself in the narrative once more, her thoughts kept drifting. The book was a comforting escape, yet something else—a persistent, unspoken concern—began to overshadow the solace it offered.

Sophia's eyes lingered on her phone, a faint reflection of the ocean's blue hue visible on the screen. Suddenly, the device vibrated, its familiar ringtone breaking the mid-morning silence. *Jazmin*—the name of her eldest daughter—flashed across the screen, and a warm smile tugged at Sophia's lips. She placed her book gently on the nearby stool and quickly swiped to answer.

Leaning back into the plush cushions of her lounge chair, Sophia felt a wave of joy as Jazmin's face filled the screen. Her daughter's smile was as bright as the Cabo sun filtering through the windows, and she waved with the enthusiasm that always made Sophia's heart swell.

"How are you doing, Mom?" Jazmin's voice crackled slightly, the connection not quite as clear as Sophia would have liked.

"I'm fine," Sophia replied, her voice calm and reassuring.

"I miss you, Mom. I hope you're not feeling lonely," Jazmin said, her concern palpable even across the distance.

"I'm alright. Always alright," Sophia answered, the words automatic, almost rehearsed.

Sophia tilted her head to the left, causing her long blonde hair to cascade over her brow.

"Did you just have your hair done?" Jazmin asked, her eyes narrowing as she examined her mother's appearance.

"No, I'm waiting for Josh to come into town to do it for me," Sophia said, fingers absentmindedly playing with a loose strand. Her hand lingered, slowly smoothing the tendrils as a faint, thoughtful smile touched her lips. Josh was one of her best friends and neighbors in Cabo, and she loved it when he came into town.

"Are you sure you're fine, Mom?" Jazmin's tone was laced

with worry, her eyes scanning the background of Sophia's living room, searching for any sign that something might be amiss.

"I'm fine. Don't worry about me," Sophia insisted, though her gaze momentarily drifted toward the ocean outside, as if seeking reassurance from it.

"You look like you've been thinking a lot. Have you been seeing anyone?" Jazmin's question hung in the air, filled with both curiosity and a hint of playful teasing.

"Oh, come on. Don't ask me that question. I've been like this for a long while. I'm sixty-five, for crying out loud. I don't have a problem with living alone," Sophia responded, her voice laced with amusement.

"I know, but I see something in your eyes, Mom," Jazmin said, her voice lowering as if sharing a secret.

"What do you see?" Sophia asked, raising an eyebrow, her expression caught between scepticism and curiosity.

"The desire to love again. I think it's healthy, and I think it would be really great if you found someone," Jazmin replied, her words carrying a weight that made Sophia pause.

"You really have that much trust in what you see in my eyes?" Sophia asked, pressing her lips together in a tight line, trying to keep her emotions in check.

"Yes. You're more than capable. I believe that's a very positive sign," Jazmin responded, her confidence unwavering.

Sophia nodded, though she didn't dwell on her daughter's observation. Her gaze shifted to the background behind Jazmin, where a familiar wedding picture hung on the wall—a reminder of a love that had weathered many storms.

"How about you, Jazmin? Has everything been good with

David? And how are the girls?" Sophia asked, her voice softening as she shifted the conversation away from herself.

"Yes. We learn new ways to love each other every day. They're great, busy with soccer and volleyball," Jazmin responded, her smile returning.

"There's no better way to sustain love. Please give them my love," Sophia said, her heart swelling with pride.

As the call ended, Sophia slowly rose from her lounge chair, the sunlight casting a warm glow on her petite frame. She locked her fingers together and stretched them upward, standing on her toes as she luxuriated in the satisfying snaps of her joints and back.

With a sense of renewed energy, Sophia walked around the living room, her hands resting on her hips as she took in the view outside. After a few moments, she returned to her lounge chair, picked up her book, and once again tried to immerse herself in its pages.

An hour later, Sophia picked up her phone and thumbed down to the Over50 app. She took a glimpse at the red icon of the app before clicking on it. Her friend Elli talked her into getting on Over50. Elli was the kind of friend Sophia had known forever, the one who could finish her sentences and remember the details even Sophia had forgotten. They'd shared everything over the years—secrets, heartbreaks, and laughter over countless glasses of wine. It was Elli, with her no-nonsense attitude and relentless optimism, who convinced Sophia to give online dating a try

Directed into the app, Sophia realized that she hadn't received a match since she registered the previous day.

"Maybe it takes a bit of time for everything to settle in," she said, out loud.

She left the lounge chair and went to the kitchen. Sophia microwaved three rolls of pastries and helped herself to a glass of lemonade from the refrigerator.

She returned to the lounge chair, which was stationed close to the windows that overlooked the bay. From the lounge chair, Sophia looked toward the glass table and four couches weaved across it in the living room.

She hadn't sat on the couches for more than a week. If she wasn't spending time in her bedroom, Sophia was in the lounge chair reading a book or sorting out a real estate document.

Sophia took a sip of lemonade and realized that her phone screen was on. She saw a text from Elli.

Don't forget our date today. 4PM.
Alexanders on the marina.

Sophia smiled and started typing a response to Elli. As she was typing, she received a notification from Over50. It read: *You Have a New Match.*

Sophia swiped off the notification and continued typing her response to Elli.

Of course, how can I forget? And please bring the Green Mile along with you. I want to start reading it once I'm done with this one.

After she sent the message, Sophia took a gulp of lemonade and clicked on the Over50 app.

She started examining her match. Sophia was captured by his gentle-looking face and his dark hair with faint gray streaks. He had an innocuous smile in all his pictures on display.

Sophia checked out his brown eyes and a sweeping, dark moustache. There were clear signs that he had a solid figure and thick, strong arms. Also, he looked quite tall, which appealed to Sophia.

Sophia was thoughtful and imagined a life with this new man. She had to take a glance at his name to augment her imagination.

"Rex Presley," she said, in a soft, thoughtful tone. "What do you have for me, Rex?"

Sophia had a smile on her face as she shaved off this thought, unwilling to be carried away by her new match. There was no message yet from him, and it made Sophia wonder whether she needed to wait or take the initiative to send the first message.

While this thought tarried in her mind, Sophia started reading Rex's bio.

I am a rancher in San Angelo, Texas. I love to Hunt and fish, and I have been doing this for a long time. I have a large ranch and in tune with nature. I don't know what else to write. Okay. I am also divorced, and I am looking for someone who favors communication and believes that communicating issues is the first step to resolving them.

Sophia didn't know what to say about Rex's bio, but she had a feeling that his writing matched his look. In any case, Sophia wondered if Rex had suffered from a lack of communication in his previous relationship.

"What sort of a man are you?" Sophia asked, thoughtfully.

She was still waiting for his message, sticking with the instructions she had received from Elli about the app. Of course, she could send the first message, but Elli had made it clear that it made more sense for the person who matched last to send the first message.

It was a bit confusing for Sophia, who didn't have any problem sending the first message. She looked at the message space for a while and picked up her glass of lemonade. She took a drink, dropped the glass, and picked up her book.

Sophia read through two lines of her book before she picked up her phone again. She clicked on the Over50 app and reread the description she had left about herself. It was pretty straightforward. She had indicated that she was a mother of three, a grandmother of three, a widow, and a real estate broker.

Sophia hadn't left a lot of information about herself or what she wanted from a match, but she reckoned it was the best way to find the right match. Since it was easy for people to pretend, Sophia didn't want a situation where a match created the impression that he was imbued with the qualities she desired in a man.

Sophia went back to drinking her lemonade and eating her pastries while she waited for Rex's message. She was also reading her book but lacked the focus she had utilized before matching with Rex.

Sophia was leaning toward the thought that Rex could be new to the app and didn't know how to go about it.

"I am new to the app, too," she said, putting off any light from this line of thought.

Perhaps he is still deliberating on my description, Sophia thought, and continued reading.

Slowly, she became aligned with the stability that highlighted the moments before matching with Rex. She took measured sips of lemonade as she read.

Suddenly, she heard a notification from her phone. It was from Over50. She picked up her phone and found that Rex had messaged her.

> Hello. So, the craziest thing happened after I matched you. A cow on my ranch went into labor. I had to immediately focus on her. I hope you are fine, Rex said

Sophia was smiling as she read the message. She nodded, dropped her glass of lemonade, and sat up in her lounge chair.

> I am fine. Really fine, but I am wondering if the cow is alright. Was it a successful delivery?

Sophia asked.

Yes. Yes. It was successful, thank you. But I am wondering if it is a good sign. I mean it's not every day a cow gives birth when you are staring at the pictures of a beautiful woman, Rex said.

Sophia smiled and shook her head. She took a moment to think about her next response.

Well, we must find out for ourselves. But you sound like you have a good head on your shoulders, Sophia responded.

Rex sent a smiling emoji, and Sophia genuinely smiled after seeing it. She went back to view his pictures, placing special attention on his eyes and mustache.

I hope so. I haven't had any luck since I registered last Saturday,

Rex said.

How many people have you matched?

Sophia asked.

Three ladies, including you. The other women were younger, so their expectations were a little out of tune,

Rex said.

Sophia nodded, taking a sip of lemonade. She looked at the

glass, shook her head, and stood up. She went to the refrigerator, refilled the glass, and returned to the lounge chair.

Tell me about your other matches,

Sophia said.

She was curious and intent on knowing the qualities of the other ladies that came as an assault on his sensibilities.

Well, the first one immediately told me she has four small children and wants a man who would raise them through high school and college. I have never seen anything so crazy. The three fathers of her children are still alive,

Rex said.

Sophia spat out blobs of lemonade after reading his message. She laughed, in disbelief. It was the funniest thing she had read all week.

Is this a joke? Are you trying to make me laugh? Well, you've succeeded.

After sending the message, Sophia reread Rex's message and started laughing again. She screenshot the message, intent on showing it to Elli when they met later in the evening.

I am not joking. You know, I asked her if she was joking because she sent it before we'd had any real conversation. To be honest, I thought it was a joke until she made it clear that it was why she joined the app. I think she was carried away by her looks. I wished her all the best and quickly unmatched,

Rex said.

He sent a laughing emoji after his message. Sophia was already chuckling as she read his message. Something about the way he conveyed them expressed his healthy sense of humor.

How about your second match?

Sophia asked, curious.

She dropped her glass of lemonade beside the book on the stool and stretched out her legs as she lay on her back. She was gritting slightly, expecting another round of humor.

The second one was even worse. You know, for a moment, I thought I was cursed,

Rex said, sending a tired emoji after his message.

Sophia had a big smile on her face, nodding as she kept her eyes on her phone screen.

Tell me about it,

she said.

She said she liked my mustache. I thought it was a great compliment until she added that it made her remember her life as a man. You know, I was confused. I thought she was talking about reincarnation, but she told me she was a transgender female. I was shocked, but I didn't think it made sense to be disappointed since she was obviously doing what she wants with her life. But then she dropped the real bomb,"

Rex said.

Tell me more,

Sophia responded.

She said she wanted a transgender man. She wanted a man that has transitioned from a woman, and she believed that I looked like one,

Rex said.

Sophia dropped her phone on her thigh and laughed loudly, clapping her hands as tears gradually welled up in her eyes.

She tried to reread the message, but her vision was blurry because of the tears in her eyes. Sophia wiped off her tears with the back of her palm and took several deep breaths. She read the message halfway and started laughing again.

Sophia's eyes were constricted as she laughed and tried to stop herself.

“This is crazy,” she said, and snuck a sip of lemonade.

Are you still there?

Rex asked.

Yes. Yes. I am still here. I don’t know what to say about your experience, but they made me laugh. I can’t believe you really experienced this. It is crazy. I would have deleted the app if my first two experiences were like this,

Sophia responded.

To be honest, I thought about deleting the app. In fact, I told myself that I would delete it if my third experience went the same way,

Rex said.

So, what’s your feeling so far?

Sophia asked.

You’ve already done more than the last two matches I had. So, I guess I’m feeling great,

Rex responded.

Your experience is probably the funniest thing I have heard this year,

Sophia said.

You know, I looked in the mirror. I wanted to see if there was something on my face that appealed to those weird folks,

Rex responded.

Again, Sophia laughed. She hadn't laughed so much in a long while, and it wasn't just Rex's story that was funny. It was the way he conveyed them. Sophia could imagine the look on his face and the tone of his voice. She could imagine Rex staring in the mirror and touching his mustache, checking out his cheeks, and wondering about the part of his face that created the impression that he used to be a woman.

Sophia could imagine him having a drink with his friends and holding forth about the crazy dating pool. She could imagine his friends laughing at him and taking a thorough look at his face to find a bit of femininity behind his mustache and brown eyes.

Sophia took a gulp of lemonade and sat back in the lounge chair. She was still reeling from Rex's terrible experience.

At least you have something you can laugh about in your spare time. How do you manage your ranch? Do you work on it alone? So, do you spend most of your time there?

Sophia asked.

I have two employees. They come three times a week, but I do most of the work. My house is on the ranch. So, it is part of my life to be honest,

Rex responded.

Sophia nodded. She wasn't sure what to make of this detail.

You must be a workaholic,

Sophia said.

Yeah. Kinda. My father was a great rancher before his death. He was a great fella and I learned so much from him. But my son, Allen, doesn't want to be a rancher. He is a hunting and fishing guide. He is doing pretty well,

Rex said.

Great. You must have raised him well,

Sophia complimented.

Yeah. He has a good life. Since his mother left us for another man when he was 8, my dating life hasn't been great. I never remarried. I fought for custody and won, dedicating most of my time to raising my son. I thank God for my family- they played a significant role in helping me as a single dad. The divorce was hard on both Allen and me, but I feel like I am ready to find love again,

Rex said.

Sophia had a serious expression on her face as she read his message. She nodded, perceiving the emotion and sincerity in his message. She took a deep breath and started rethinking her desire to recommit to a relationship.

Since she hadn't been in one since the death of her husband, Sophia didn't know what to expect. She was torn between living the rest of her life alone and finding someone who matched her desires and connected strongly with her values.

I see that you are a widow. I am sorry about that. I am really hoping you are doing ok,

Rex said.

I am doing good. It happened several years ago. Yes. I wish it didn't happen; life can be so cruel at times. To be honest, I have gotten really used to my own company. I think it makes me really ready to share my space with a companion,

Sophia said.

You couldn't be more right,

Rex responded, adding a smiling emoji at the end of his message.

In the evening, Sophia drove down the long highway along the ocean. The ambience was cool, and the iridescent buildings along the road were complemented by the presence of tourists.

Sophia drove slowly, fawning over the couples in her line of vision, how they held hands, took snapshots of themselves, and immersed themselves in the spirit of love. It was one of the perks she considered before relocating from the US to Mexico.

The mix of different languages in the air piled together into a cacophonous beat. The sounds of a variety of music seeped out from bars with tiny doors.

Sophia met straw-hat-wearing ladies dancing inside a bar with transparent glass walls. She met a magician in denim-blue jeans and a tucked-in vintage shirt, speaking quickly in Spanish as he carved out another round of magic.

Moments later, Sophia pulled up outside Solomon's Landing- the restaurant had the most beautiful views of the marina.

Inside, Sophia walked to Elli's table and gave her a warm embrace. Elli placed one hand on Sophia's shoulder and took a long look at her off-the-shoulder dress and black pump shoes.

"How do you always find a way to look so gorgeous?" Elli asked, exuding an impressed smile.

Sophia looked from Elli's black hair, which was tied in a bun, to her face imbued with high-laying cheekbones.

"You're one to talk. You always look amazing."

Elli chuckled. "We could go back and forth on this forever, but let's not."

They settled into their seats. Elli reached into her black bag and handed Sophia a book. "Here's *The Green Mile.* Careful with this one—it brought tears to my eyes."

Sophia took the book, glancing at the cover. "If it made you cry, it must be something special."

A waiter approached, preparing a tableside Caesar salad and setting down two glasses of wine. "You know me too well," Sophia said, watching him work.

Elli grinned. "What else would you eat here?"

As they started on their salads, Sophia hesitated before speaking. "I matched with someone today on Over50."

Elli paused, then raised an eyebrow. "Oh? And what's he like?"

Sophia pulled out her phone, showing Elli pictures of Rex. Elli studied them, her expression thoughtful.

"He seems really easygoing," Elli said carefully. "But remember, it's just a match. Don't get your hopes up too soon."

Sophia shrugged, taking a sip of her wine. "I know. But it's nice to feel a connection again, even if it's just the start. And he's *really* funny."

Elli sighed, her voice softening. "I just want you to be careful, Sophia. These things can be unpredictable."

Sophia smiled, appreciating Elli's concern. "I know. But sometimes, you just have to see where things go."

A beat passed before Sophia asked, "How's Frank?"

Elli nodded, then leaned back in her chair. "Frank's doing fine—though sometimes I wonder if he's cheating on me."

Sophia raised an eyebrow. "Frank? Cheating on you? At his age?"

Elli laughed, shaking her head. "You'd be surprised. Men these days take all sorts of things to keep themselves going. A nurse at the clinic told me that even older guys are getting injections to get their thing up."

Sophia chuckled, trying to imagine it. "You're exaggerating."

"Maybe, but you can never be too sure. I trust Frank, but sometimes I wonder what he was up to when he traveled so much early in our marriage."

"Frank's a good man, Elli. You've been together for thirty years, and you're still going strong."

Elli smiled, a soft look in her eyes. "Yeah, I guess I'm just paranoid. He's still the man of my dreams, after all these years."

"See? You're lucky to have him," Sophia said, her tone more serious. "Not everyone finds that kind of love."

Elli nodded, her expression thoughtful. "True. But don't forget, I had to work on him—anoint him with some oil, cast out a few demons." She winked, laughing.

Sophia laughed along with her, then teased, "Well, at least you don't think all men are dogs anymore."

Elli smirked, shaking her head. "Oh, they're still dogs, Sophia. But they're more than that—complicated creatures we can't help but want."

Sophia rolled her eyes, smiling. "You're impossible."

"Maybe. But if you start dating again, you might need some of that oil too," Elli teased.

Sophia shook her head, smiling as she took another sip of her wine.

"So, if everything goes to plan, where do you see yourself

with Rex? Are we looking at a second marriage? Is it just going to be a short fling?" Elli fixed her eyes on Sophia after asking this question.

Sophia sat back, pressing her lips together. "I don't know. I guess we just have to see how it goes," she responded, hopefully.

Later that night, Sophia made a meal of pasta and sauce. She was in the kitchen when it occurred to her that she hadn't reached out to Rex despite promising to do so after her date with Elli. She returned to the living room, picked up her phone from the stool beside the lounge chair, and saw a message from Rex on Over50. She clicked on the message and took a deep breath.

Are you alright?

Was it supposed to be a long date?

Please let me know that you are okay.

Sophia realized that Rex sent a message every twenty-five minutes. Sophia had a feeling that Rex was truly concerned and worried.

I am fine. I am really fine. It was a great date, to be honest. Ellie is very funny, and she has a reputation for saying things that can annoy the heart but contain a lot of truth.

After responding to Rex's messages, Sophia felt something was missing. She started typing again.

I am sorry for not letting you know that I have returned. It skipped me. I hope you're fine.

Sophia felt slightly relieved after sending the second message. She mingled with the thought that she had truly shown appreciation for Rex's concerns.

Sophia only needed to wait for two minutes before Rex responded to her messages.

I am really happy to hear that you are fine. I have heard lots of crazy stories about Mexico.

Sophia smiled, nodding.

The crazy things usually happen in the north. You don't see that kind of violence in Cabo. It was why I chose to live here,

Sophia replied.

Oh! Cabo. I have heard a fair bit about that place. I think a friend was talking about how good the fishing was there,

Rex said.

Sophia nodded, a smile creeping up her face.

Yes. We have lots of good fishing here in Cabo. We also have a lot of whales. Whale season is my favorite time of year.

Sophia sat back in the lounge chair, immersing herself in the conversation.

Have you always lived there?

Rex asked.

No. I was living in the US until three years ago. I decided to retire here. It's been a long time coming.

Great. Well, I just finished making a beef roast. I think it is the best I have had in a long time,

Rex said.

Sophia chuckled slightly, her face beaming up. She was considerably touched by Rex's willingness to elevate his culinary skills.

You must really make great beef roasts if it is the best you've had in a long time,

Sophia responded.

If you were close by, I would have sent some your way. I'm telling you. It's really good,

Rex said, sending a winking emoji afterward.

Sophia chuckled for a while before suddenly taking a serious expression. It started to dawn on her that Rex was already leaving a great impression on her. He was boldly ticking the boxes that appealed to her, and it made it easy to think that she needed to start considering a future where he would be important.

Easily, Sophia married this line of thought with Elli's fervent observation and warnings. She took a deep breath and started typing.

> I think you're really funny Rex. And being a good cook myself, I really think cooking can be our thing. But I am wondering if you would mind a video call. I would like to see who I'm speaking with.

After sending the message, Sophia's palpitation gathered pace. She was slightly anxious. She took several deep breaths and dropped her phone on her thigh.

She sat up in the lounge chair and closed her eyes. Internally, she made herself believe that she would keep her eyes closed until an Over50 notification from her phone.

Four minutes later, Sophia opened her eyes. The notification had not come. She tried not to think too much about it. Whenever her mind flirted with the thought of Rex's behavior, Sophia distracted herself with the memory of the meeting with Elli.

Nonetheless, she had a serious expression, leaving hints of her gradual flow towards resignation.

Sophia stood up from the lounge chair and took her phone to the dining table. She dropped her phone on the table and opened a bottle of wine. She filled an empty glass halfway and sat in a cushioned straight-back chair at the head of the table.

Sophia took a sip of wine and smiled. It was hard to determine the rationale behind her smile, but Sophia kept it there like bad weather.

She took another sip of wine, her expression tightened, and her palpitation became settled. It appeared she was making peace with Rex's disappearing act.

She took another sip. The third sip of wine drowned out her serious expression, leaving a normal, ponderous look. Sophia looked toward the lounge and thought about continuing from where she left off in her reading. *The Perks of Being a Wallflower* was on the stool.

As Sophia stood up, her phone beeped. The sound sent a wave of warmth through her stomach, causing her to release a loud sigh. The notification was from Over50. Sophia clicked on it and found a message from Rex:

> Hey. I had to go change. I need to look my best, you know. I am ready now. Come on.

A smiling emoji followed his message, and Sophia had a big smile on her face as she reached for the video call icon.

She dropped back in her chair, took a sip of wine, and tapped on the button.

Rex answered quickly, his mustache appearing on the screen before he shifted back and showed his face clearly.

He waved at Sophia, his face brightening up.

"Hi," he said.

CHAPTER 2
Late Night Chats

On this particular night, Sophia was sitting at the dining table after eating a meal of poblano chicken. She had a glass of wine on the table, a book, and her phone, and was engulfed in a heated, vibrant aura.

Her hand kept grazing her phone until she picked it up and took a look at the time. It was edging past nine-forty PM in the night. She took a sip of wine and browsed across Facebook. She noticed a comment from Jazmin on a photo she recently saw on Facebook. Elli had posted a photo she took had taken of them on the Marina.

> Hey! Mom. You are looking as sharp as ever. How do you manage to look younger and beautiful every day?

The comment left a smile on Sophia's face.

She quickly responded to the comment:

You and your siblings are my secret, Jazmin. To be loved by you is a blessing I don't take for granted.

After leaving the response, tears started to well up in Sophia's eyes. She started to think about the way she had helped infuse love in the hearts of her children and fostered a close-knit family.

In that moment, she received an iMessage from Rex:

Hey love! The outing with Roger was a delight. We talked a great deal. I am not sure we've ever spent so much time talking than drinking.

Sophia took a sip of wine before responding.

It must have been an interesting conversation. What were you guys talking about?

Sophia checked back on Facebook and discovered that Jazmin had left a love reaction to her comment.

Also, Elli had left a comment: *Look at my girl! The goddess of Cabo.*

Sophia chuckled and shook her head. "Elli," she said, smiling.

She started typing a reply.

Don't flatter me, Elli. You are the true goddess of Cabo.

After leaving the reply on to Elli's comment, a message from Rex popped up on her phone:

> Honestly, we talked a great deal about you. Roger is actually surprised that I am dating a lady from Over50. He didn't think the app worked like that. I told him you are the most precious lady I have spoken to. He thinks I'm crazy and love-struck and wants me to wait to experience you in person so I don't get disappointed, but honestly, I don't think that's an issue. Roger doesn't believe in virtual connection. In fact, he doesn't think the virtual world is real.

Sophia nodded and started typing a response:

> To be honest, there have been times I felt we were moving at a fast pace. I have never really been into anyone so quickly. How long has it been? Fourteen days? It is slightly crazy.

A smile crept across Sophia's face after she sent the message. Rex responded quickly:

> To be honest, I don't think I can have a good or productive day if I don't hear from you. It is that intense for me.

Sophia's smile broadened. Since her growing influence on Rex was reciprocated by his influence on her, Sophia believed that they were moving at a pace that highlighted equality in vulnerability and intensity.

I would easily say the same about myself. I think those crazy Over50 experiences prepared you for me.

This time, Sophia left a smiling emoji after her message.

Ah! Those crazy experiences. I still can't believe they happened, you know. Even Roger thinks they are crazy.

Sophia took a sip of wine and saw a notification on her screen, indicating a response from Elli. When she checked, Sophia discovered that Elli had simply responded with a sticker. It was a sticker of Jim Carrey making a funny face.

Sophia laughed because she imagined Elli making her face that way. Afterward, she left a laughing reaction to the comment.

What are you up to tonight?

Rex asked.

Nothing really. I am halfway through The Green Mile. It is a wonderful book by the way. How often do you get to read?

Sophia asked.

Not so much to be honest, but I follow the news. Also, I read comments and articles on Facebook. They can be crazy and thought-provoking at times,

Rex responded.

Alright then. I made poblano chicken for dinner. It was wonderful,

Sophia said.

Please send the recipe. I'd like to try it,

Rex responded.

Sophia smiled, impressed. She took a sip of wine and stood up from the chair, leaving the glass of wine on the table.

This one is really simple. You tenderize and season your chicken breast and dredge them in flour before frying. Then you make a cream sauce with poblano peppers, put it all together and bake for 20 minutes,

Sophia responded.

She walked towards the lounge chair and around the living room. She stretched her hands upward, tightening her grip on her phone.

After a brief pause, Sophia sat in the lounge chair and raised her two legs up, moving them slowly.

She was apt to indulge in these routine exercises after sitting in a particular spot for a long period.

> I can't believe you think this recipe is simple to implement. I think I'd need all my patience for this one,

Rex responded.

Sitting back in the lounge chair, Sophia typed back a response:

> You'll get really creamy and flavorful chicken, but don't get too used to it. I haven't had poblano chicken in a year. I don't think it is very healthy, but you are a workaholic. So you probably don't have to worry so much about it.

Sophia started moving her legs quickly as she arched them upward. Her phone beeped, signifying a response from Rex, but Sophia continued moving her legs.

Two minutes later, she dropped her legs and moved from the lounge chair. She took her phone with her as she made her way back to the dining table. After sitting back in her chair, she thumbed on her phone and found Rex's response:

> I think I'll still try it. I want to get used to what you are eating.

As Sophia smiled, she took a glance at the time on her phone screen. It was edging past eleven fifteen PM. She took her wine in two gulps and went to the bedroom.

Sophia's bedroom was a peaceful, well-kept space that carried the soothing scent of lavender. The king-sized bed, made up with crisp white linens, had a cozy white throw blanket casually draped at the foot. She'd left the balcony doors slightly open, letting in a gentle sea breeze that mingled with the room's calming fragrance.

A vase on the nightstand held a single white orchid, its simplicity matching the room's vibe. The floor was softened by a thick, cream-colored rug, which added a touch of warmth to the cool tiles beneath. Across from the bed stood a wide dresser with an antique mirror hanging above it.

The walls were painted an elegant shade of cream, adorned with a few pieces of art—mostly seascapes that reminded her of the view outside. In the corner, a plush gray armchair beckoned, a spot where she often curled up with a book before bed. The room was simple but elegant, with every detail reflecting Sophia's personality.

You are working on your ranch tomorrow morning, right? I think you mentioned it this afternoon,

Sophia asked.

Yeah. I should probably catch some sleep,

Rex replied.

You really should. I want to take a shower before catching some sleep,

Sophia said.

Okay then. Goodnight. I love you,

Rex responded.

Sophia took a long look at his message and dropped down in her bed. Her eyes were fixated on the part where it said he loved her. It was the first time Rex had used those words in their conversations, but the nature of their conversations, the way they flowed, and the feelings that tarried in her heart already expressed her growing love for him.

Nonetheless, Sophia had been reluctant to use those words. Of course, she thought about him every day, and with the trajectory of their relationship, Sophia believed that she was growing closer and closer to him. Hence, I love you was something she had always said in her heart. It was the band that tied them together. It was the wave that carried them to the coastline of happiness and compatibility.

I love you too, Rex. Please sleep well.

After sending the message, a shiver ran up her spine. The pace of their relationship was amazing, and since Sophia hadn't been in a relationship since her husband's death, she wondered if she was being a bit naive with Rex.

She moved into the bathroom and stood underneath the shower, drenching herself in cold water as she looked through the small bathroom window. There was a gibbous moon in the clear sky, and for a moment, Sophia felt like the moon was looking back at her and indulging the intensity of her relationship with Rex.

Elli came over on Saturday, donning a blue dress and allowing her dark, long hair to cascade down her back.

She went for the wine on the dining table and filled her glass to the brim. She traipsed down to the kitchen and stood at the door, watching as Sophia put the finishing touches on her famous baked brie with roasted garlic.

Sophia took out the pan from the oven and turned out the browned baked brie on a flat ceramic plate. She turned to the door and met Elli, sneaking a sip of wine while she looked toward her.

Sophia placed the roasted garlic and the crackers on the ceramic plate.

"You are so good at this, you know. Anyone will be happy to have you," Elli complimented, helping herself to the brie.

Together, they moved to the dining table. Sophia brought another bottle of wine.

She served her glass of wine, took a sip, and sat beside Elli.

Elli spread a piece of the roasted garlic onto a cracker, topped it with some brie and shoved it into her mouth. She nodded as she masticated noiselessly.

"This is really good. Why haven't you thought about opening a restaurant?"

"Are you serious?" Sophia asked.

"Of course! You could retire doing what you love."

"Running a restaurant is real work, Elli. I don't need that stress, especially with so many good restaurants here in Cabo."

"You don't think you could compete?"

Sophia shook her head. "It's just not on my agenda."

Elli snapped a picture of her plate, holding her wine glass above it. "What are you up to?" Sophia asked.

"Just sending this to Frank. He's missing out."

"You're up to something," Sophia teased.

"Maybe," Elli winked. "I bet he'll be jealous of your culinary skills."

Sophia laughed. "You're crazy. He already knows."

"Yeah, but seeing is believing." Elli sent the picture and pulled out a book. "Got this for you. I think you'll like it."

Sophia glanced at the cover. "The Notebook" was boldly inscribed on the cover.

"Looks like a romance."

"It's perfect now that you're in love with Rex," Elli teased. "You're giving us that Romeo and Juliet vibe at sixty-five."

Sophia blushed slightly. "What Rex and I have is different. It's mature, committed."

Elli nodded, taking a sip of wine. "Love makes us all act like kids. It's part of the fun."

Sophia rolled her eyes, smiling. "Where do you get this stuff? Is it the book?"

"It's not the book," Elli said, gesturing to the novel. "It's just experience. Love can be complicated, but it doesn't have to be."

Sophia considered this. "So, you don't take life too seriously?"

"I take myself seriously, not the world. What's to lose? At the end of the day, it's about the people who matter."

"Is that why you were worried when I mentioned Rex?"

Elli sighed. "I just didn't want you to overestimate his role in your life. But I see it's different with him. You've got a good thing."

Sophia smiled. "I think so too."

Elli's phone beeped, and she laughed. "It's Frank. He's

throwing a fit because I sent that picture. He's upset I might finish all the brie."

Sophia grinned. "I'll give you some to take home."

"No way. I want to rub it in. He does the same to me."

Sophia chuckled. "Okay, but don't go too hard on him."

"This is a battle, Sophia. Be on my side!" Elli said theatrically.

Sophia shook her head, still smiling. "I can't stop eating this brie."

"Don't start," Sophia warned, frowning playfully.

"Start what?"

"You know what."

"You really should open a restaurant," Elli chuckled.

Sophia spent the evening on her bed, FaceTiming with Rex. Her room was resplendent, and she wore a red nightdress.

Sophia reclined against the head of her bed, drawing her white duvet to her stomach.

Rex was smiling as he walked around his bachelor pad home. It was a rectangular, sprawling space, but Sophia had her eyes on the austere features and how the design of the room hindered its potential.

Rex walked to the far wall, which was draped over with thick, opaque glass. He sat in an adjustable chair and placed his legs on a stool. He was holding a cup of tea in one hand, and a bright smile touched his face.

"How was your day?" Rex asked.

"It was great. Spent it with Elli. She brought me a new book."

"Sounds fun. I spent the day clearing some fields," Rex said, taking a sip of tea.

"Must be hard work."

"It is, but it's rewarding. You look stunning tonight," Rex added, his eyes admiring her.

"Thank you," Sophia replied, blushing.

"Do you ever think about the future?" Rex asked, a hint of seriousness in his voice.

"All the time."

"Do you see me in it?"

"You're part of my life now, so yes, you're in my future."

Rex smiled, his expression softening. "I've been dreaming about you lately. In one, you handed me a rose at my ranch."

"That's sweet," Sophia said, smiling.

Rex's tone grew somber. "I didn't think I'd be in another relationship after how my last one ended. My son, Allen, encouraged me not to give up on love, even though he never liked my ex. She was troubled. Loved true crime shows, but not in a healthy way. She'd wake up screaming, then apologize like nothing happened."

"That sounds intense," Sophia said, her focus entirely on him.

"It was. I knew I didn't love her it was just for companionship. But somehow, it wasn't enough, you know. If she couldn't get hold of me, she would call my neighbors to see if they could go over and see if my truck was in the driveway at the ranch. One night she came over shouting at me and saying all kinds of crazy stuff. She said that if I wasn't going to marry her she was going to find someone that would. And she was apparently already seeing another guy," Rex said, taking a deep breath. He had a sad smile on his face. "My family did not like her and Roger surely didn't either. I knew then I couldn't keep going. I asked her to leave, but she kept coming back, apologizing, trying to make things right. But it never felt right.."

Sophia's heart ached for him. "It's okay, Rex. You don't have to go on if it's too much."

"No, I want to. I feel safe talking to you." He took a deep breath. "I finally ended it and got a restraining order. Even then, she showed up, wanting to stay friends. It was exhausting."

"Does she still live in San Angelo? Have you run into her?" Sophia asked, concerned.

"Occasionally, with her new guy. I avoid them. I regret ever meeting her, but maybe I had to go through that to find you."

Sophia nodded. "Maybe we wouldn't have met if you hadn't gone through that. Life has a strange way of working out."

"Yeah," Rex agreed, his voice filled with emotion. "Thank you, Sophia, for bringing warmth back into my life."

Sophia smiled, locking eyes with him. "You're welcome."

CHAPTER 3

Virtual Dates

Sophia woke to sunlight streaming through her window. Squinting, she rolled out of bed and closed the curtains. Stretching her arms and legs, she enjoyed the satisfying snap of her muscles. After a few more stretches, she moved into a rigorous workout, leaving her sweaty and drained. A cold shower refreshed her, and once dressed in a white dress, she checked her phone, finding a morning text from Jazmin.

> Stay strong, Mom. I love you so much. Whenever I try to confront an issue, I try to wonder how you would react to it. Thank you for teaching me to be strong. Are you feeling lonely? Hope you know you can talk to me.

Sophia smiled through the message until she reached Jazmin's question. Her question made her take a deep breath. She moved with her phone to the kitchen, checking out the chicken breast she had seasoned and tenderized.

Sophia loved making chicken poblano, and Rex wouldn't stop talking about it, so they decided to go on a virtual date today.

As she checked the chicken thighs, her phone started ringing. She answered quickly and saw that Rex was also standing in the kitchen of his home. He had a big smile on his face as he stretched the bowl of tenderized chicken to the camera.

Sophia was infected by his smile.

She instructed him to dredge the chicken in flour.

Rex was focused, following her instructions. Sophia took a peek at him as she busied herself with preparing her own poblano chicken. She saw a bottle of wine and glass on his living room table.

Rex dropped the plate of dredged chicken beside the bottle and turned to Sophia.

"Are you ready?" she asked.

"Yeah. Are we still watching *Fight Club*? Roger recommended it," Rex responded.

"Yes, I checked it out. I think it is going to be an interesting movie."

"I can't wait to watch it with you," Rex responded.

After the chicken was ready, Sophia went to sit on her living room couch. She chose the longest couch because its position overlooked the TV.

It was the first time Sophia had spent time on her couch for a long time. Since she wasn't so into movies, Sophia took some time to really focus on the movie.

She took infrequent side looks at her phone, checking out Rex's expression. He had a calm, observant look.

At one point, they locked eyes. Rex winked and took a bite

of his chicken. He took a sip of wine and went back to watching TV.

Sophia's eyes were on the TV. She had a glass of wine in one hand but struggled to fully detach herself from her mind. She was thinking about Jazmin's text and realized she needed to take her time to let her children in on the intense development in her love life.

"Are you enjoying the movie?" Rex asked, jolting her from her thoughts.

She turned to the phone screen, smiled, and nodded.

"That guy is really a psycho. Maybe the ultimate psycho," he commented. "Do you think it is possible for people to lead two lives in that manner?" Rex added.

"I don't know, but I have read a few psychology texts that harped on the issue. I think multiple personality disorder is not a myth," she said.

"Wow. It is crazy. You know, it is making me wonder," he added as an afterthought.

"Maybe your ex even had it. It was really crazy to behave the way she did, don't you think?" Sophia asked.

Rex tilted his face up slightly and nodded his head.

"I think you have a point. I mean, I didn't really see it that way, but I don't think it is like the guy in this movie. She was definitely crazy. In fact, I don't think it was really a disorder. She is just crazy," Rex responded, picking up his empty plate and waving it at Sophia.

"This was really delicious," Rex said, dropping the plate.

Sophia picked up her plate. She had only eaten two pieces of chicken.

"What are you waiting for?" Rex asked.

"Well, I don't eat too much at a time."

"Sounds like you don't eat at all," Rex said, taking another look at the plate. "Okay. You really said you don't like having chicken so often."

"Yes. I said that, but I wouldn't have eaten so quickly at any point, to be honest. But I will try and finish it today."

"Should we watch another movie?" Rex asked.

"I hope you won't be bored since you have finished your chicken," Sophia responded.

"No. How can I be bored when I have you around?" Rex asked. "I hope you don't mind Roger's recommendations. I can see that most of the movies he recommended were old."

"No. Old movies are great."

"So, are we watching Gladiator next?" Rex asked.

"Okay."

While they watched the movie, Sophia received a text from Elli, but she ignored it because she had already informed her that her afternoon and evening would be spent on a virtual date with Rex.

She sat back on the couch and wondered whether Elli was having an emergency. Sophia picked up her phone and checked the text.

> I hope you are having a great time. I am rooting for you.

Sophia smiled and turned back to the TV. Rex was focused, interested.

Sophia took a brief look at his mustache and followed the undulation of his lips and how they were carved out thoughtfully.

"They are so kissable," she said and quickly pressed her lips together.

Rex turned to his phone screen and gave her a curious look. "Did you say something?" he asked.

"It was just a thought," Sophia responded, smiling.

Rex nodded and went back to watching the movie. At some point in the movie, Sophia became emotional. Tears welled up in her eyes and she seemed completely absorbed in the emotional atmosphere of the movie.

Her mind wandered, reiterating the importance of family. Without the presence of her children, Sophia reckoned she would have struggled to cope with grief from losing her husband.

Grief, at that point, took a room in her heart. It became a living thing in her eyes, an important figure that constantly took a seat beside her. Grief took a space in her bed and embraced her whenever she was alone.

She knew she was better because grief was no longer felt in her home. The spaces it occupied were covered by nourishment and healthy thoughts.

"I really like this one," Rex said. He had a serious, solemn look.

"I can see why Roger recommended it," Sophia responded.

"How did it make you feel?" Rex asked.

"Emotional. It touched my heart so much."

"Me too. I don't think anyone needs to go through such devastation alone," Rex added.

"You are right, but only a few of us are lucky enough to have people around us in our time of sorrow. Whether we like it or not, much of the world goes through grief alone."

Rex took a deep breath and looked like he didn't know how to respond to Sophia's utterance. He had a ponderous look and placed one hand on his face, taking a deep breath.

A transitory moment of silence came between them. Sophia had her eyes on Rex, watching as he kept scratching his low, dark hair. After a while, he started rubbing his forefinger on his mustache.

"Are you alright?" Sophia asked.

"I don't know how to tell you this, my love, but I miss you," Rex responded.

Sophia was taken aback by his response. She sat back, constricting her eyes ever so slightly.

"I don't understand. I'm right here with you," Sophia responded.

"Yeah, I know. And still, I miss you so much. I want to feel your face and your warm embrace. We have been talking for months. I think we should start considering meeting each other for the first time. What do you think?" Rex asked.

His lips quivered ever so slightly as he fixed his eyes on the screen.

Sophia was ponderous and looked slightly expressionless as she looked back at him.

Slowly, guilt crept up Rex's face. "Okay. I'm sorry. Maybe I am rushing things. Maybe we should keep taking things slow..."

"No. No. I don't think you are rushing things. We've had enough time to talk. I wasn't expecting this because I felt I might be the one to ask this question," Sophia cut in, interrupting him.

"So you have no problem with arranging a meeting?" Rex asked.

"I don't really have a problem, but I'll have to think about it and talk to my children."

"That's okay. I haven't asked because I wanted to do it at the right time. I didn't want a timeline that inconvenienced you."

"I understand. We'll just plan it like we've planned all our virtual dates," Sophia responded.

"That sounds really great. I feel really excited. I really miss you. And it's crazy. I told Roger about inviting you to Texas, and he took the deepest breath I have seen him take," Rex said.

"Why?"

"He said he is happy we have gotten to that stage, but he is just worried about me. He didn't like how much I suffered in my last relationship."

"I understand. He is just trying to protect you."

"You know, Roger accused me of falling too deeply in the pool of love. He wants me to take things easy, but how can I do that when I have you? When I feel so safe in your embrace? He said I sound like Shakespeare when I talk about you," Rex said, chuckling.

Sophia smiled and fixed her eyes on Rex's brown eyes. She had a vivid sense of the excitement that tarried inside them.

"I love the way your eyes look when you talk about me," Sophia said softly.

"Really? How do they look?"

"Appreciative. I think that is important."

"You are able to glean this from just looking into my eyes?" Rex asked.

"It is hard for eyes to lie. And I feel really loved by you. I didn't think I would ever be in this situation when I joined that app. You have opened another road that I didn't think I'd need," Sophia trilled in a soft, calming voice.

Rex nodded and kept his eyes on the screen. He looked half-closeted in his mind and kept nodding. "Although I have made a few mistakes in the past, I have a really good feeling about us. I feel we can rise and break any chain," Rex responded.

"I feel the same way too. Also, I think you have asked the right question at the right time. We should really be planning on a physical meeting," Sophia said, taking a piece of chicken from the plate on the stool beside her. "Your expressions have really opened my stomach up," she said, giggling as she took a bite of chicken.

Rex exuded a bright smile that revealed his perfect dentition.

In the evening, Sophia drove down to Elli's home in San Jose. She pulled up to the periphery of the building and heard the sound of loud music wafting up from the building.

As she clambered up the porch, Sophia heard a loud scream. It was Elli's voice, but it took a crazy, uncontrolled dimension.

Sophia didn't know whether to be concerned or take it as Elli being her usual, crazy self.

She went to the door, knocked, but didn't get a response from inside. From the sound of Elli's voice, it was easy to think that she was in the living room.

Sophia went to the side of the building and looked through one of the living room windows.

Elli was dancing with Frank. It was an intense dance that had Elli rocking her husband from behind. It was funny and cracked Sophia up.

Sophia returned to the door, knocked once, and wound down the knob. The door opened.

She crept into the living room and stood beside the door, watching Elli and Frank.

Frank was seventy-one but was able to move his feet freely. Sophia smiled and didn't want to interrupt them.

Elli made a funny twist that made her turn toward the door. Her eyes dilated.

"Sophia," she said, excitedly.

Frank straightened and turned toward the door. He sucked in his lips and stroked his brow ever so slightly. "Welcome, Sophia," he said.

"Thank you. I see you're as agile as ever," Sophia complimented.

Frank tapped his gray hair and uttered a quick smile.

"You have to keep the body moving. That's the secret," he said and started away from the living room.

"I didn't know it was time," Elli said, shaking her head.

"I can see why. You were clearly having fun. To be honest, I feel like I have interrupted something really special."

"No. Don't be like that," Elli said, wiping off beads of sweat on her brow. "You know I have cranberry juice. I should give you that first glass."

"You made it?" Sophia asked.

"Nah. I bought it," Elli responded and moved into her kitchen. She returned with a glass jug and two glasses. She quickly filled one glass halfway and handed it to Sophia.

"Thank you," Sophia said, taking the glass from her.

Elli left the living room and returned fifteen minutes later. She looked fresh and wore a black night dress. Also, she returned with a tray.

"Are those tacos?" Sophia asked.

"Yeah. You always have them when we go out," Elli responded.

"But you didn't have to buy them. You know your presence alone is enough for me," Sophia said softly.

"Yeah. But I should at least treat you the way you treat me. Not being able to cook like you is not an excuse," Elli said, taking a taco.

She took a bite. "This one is really delicious."

Sophia shook her head and took a bite from the other taco on the tray.

"How was the movie date?" Elli asked.

"It was great. Rex always has a calming presence."

"Did you guys kiss your phone screens?" Elli asked.

"I am *not* answering that question," Sophia responded, laughing.

"Lovers. Now you see how childish it can be?" Elli asked.

"You always sound like an outside spectator, but you couldn't stop rocking Frank, could you?" Sophia asked.

Ellis's eyes dilated as she giggled. "I know I wouldn't hear the end of it."

"You bet. I have a theory now."

"Interesting. I hope it isn't about me."

"Of course it is about you."

"Okay. Can we just pretend you didn't see anything? It is just one of those days. Everyone has one of those days."

"I think you have a fair bit of those days, Elli. In fact, I think most of your theories about love are based on your observation of your behavior around Frank."

"Come on. I see a lot of people. It is not just about me."

"Most. I said most. Remember how you said love makes adult children?" Sophia asked.

"Please, it is just one of those days. A dance that got out of hand."

"Why are you afraid to be a lover girl? You were rocking him so badly. Also, he was throwing tantrums after you sent him a picture of the brie I made for you two months ago."

Elli took a bite of taco and looked away from Sophia.

"So you are going to look away from me now?"

"I thought you already won. You brought a bazooka to a knife fight. What did you expect?"

"This is not about winning," Sophia responded.

"I see that already. Isn't that why you brought a bazooka?" Elli asked. "Tell me about Rex. I like your story."

"I like your story," Sophia mimicked. "You are such a child," Sophia added, giggling.

Sophia's giggling was infectious, and Elli joined in. Elli placed one hand across her lips as she giggled.

Elli looked away from Sophia and took a bite of taco. Sophia wouldn't take her eyes off her, and Elli was amused by the thought of looking toward her.

"I have decided to meet Rex," Sophia said suddenly.

Elli turned to her, dropping the half-eaten roll of taco on the tray. "Are you serious?" Elli asked.

Sophia hesitated for a split second before answering, "Yes."

"Is he coming to meet you, or you're going to meet him?" Elli asked.

"We haven't decided that yet, but I think I'd prefer to go to Texas. It will give me an opportunity to see him properly."

"Are you really sure you want to do this?"

"I couldn't be *surer*, Elli. Apart from being loved by him, I feel really appreciated," Sophia responded emotionally.

Sophia was thinking about Jazmin when she got back home. She took out her phone and reread her message before typing a response.

> If you remember clearly, I told you I was talking to a man named Rex. He lives in San Angelo. Things have really gotten intense between us. So, I am thinking about meeting him pretty soon. I feel appreciated by him and I really think I am making the right decision.

After sending the message, Sophia changed into a night dress and dropped down in her bed. She messaged Rex.

How was the rest of your day?

Sophia only needed to wait for two minutes before she received a response from Rex.

> Yeah. It was great. Roger came over. We talked about a lot of stuff. We also talked about you. I always talk about you.

Sophia smiled, delighted by Rex's response. In that moment, a message from Jazmin popped up on her phone screen.

> Are you really serious, Mom? I can't believe it. What's really special about him? How has he managed to change your decision not to try dating again? Have you seen him? I hope you are not being catfished. I have texted Jack and Sabrina. I think they are as worried as I am.

After reading Jazmin's message, Sophia received messages from Sabrina- her youngest daughter, and Jack- her son.

Sabrina sent another message in a WhatsApp family groupchat:

> Am I the only one concerned about this? Mom is usually careful about things of the heart? What has really changed?

After a while, Jack responded to Sabrina's message, following the undulation of her reservations about Sophia's relationship with Rex.

Sophia dropped her phone on the bed and went to the living room. She walked around the living room, wearing a serious expression. She was thoughtful, but she mingled with peace like a river.

Although she was dealing with a largely unfamiliar terrain, she trusted her instinct. She went back to the room, picked up her phone, and saw throngs of messages on the family WhatsApp group.

Her children were already discussing this sudden development. Sabrina held forth about the likelihood that Sophia was dealing with a man who had manipulative tendencies to say the right things.

Sophia could feel Sabrina's emotions, inlcluding fear, from her bed. Despite leaving a throng of messages on the WhatsApp group, Sabrina also sent a few more messages to her.

Sophia was patient and read through their reservations. Jack had a feeling that Sophia was becoming lonely and had fallen for Rex because he had covered the overlarge emptiness she had mingled with.

Sabrina and Jack kept exchanging their theories. Sabrina talked about visiting Cabo and staying with Sophia for a week. She wondered whether the siblings could devise a formula that could make Sophia less lonely.

Despite her feelings about Rex, Sophia appreciated their concerns. It buttressed the love and care that prevailed in her family.

Some of the messages made her smile, but she held herself back from responding. She wanted to make a timely response that covered all the issues her children had raised.

> Have you tried to call her, Jazmin? She is not replying any of my messages. Why do I have a feeling that she might already be on her way to Texas? You know how Mom can religiously follow her heart,

Sabrina asked.

Mom is not like that. She told me because she is still thinking about it. I don't think you should worry too much. I am sure Mom has seen something in him. She has always had that ability to spot certain qualities,

Jazmin responded.

But she is getting old. Age can change lots of things in a person. Even a prudent and wise person,

Sabrina said.

Let's not say too much before she replies. I am sure Mom has everything under control,

Jazmin insisted.

Sophia took a deep breath and felt the time had come to respond to her children. In that instant, a message came from Rex.

The gift of your presence cannot be overemphasized in my life. I see all the things that I have always wanted in a person when I think about you and consider how our relationship has grown over the months. You are like the breath a drowning man takes once his head is above water. You know, I told Roger that you are my salvation because you are from God.

Sophia took a deep breath, succumbing to an overwhelming rush of emotions. Internally, she felt a telepathic understanding had been initiated between Rex and her. His message, brief and poetic, vitalized her body and emboldened the feelings that tarried in her heart. It strengthened her perception of her relationship with him. And when Sophia started typing a response in the WhatsApp group, dribbles of tears gathered in her eyes.

I understand your feelings. I have taken my time to respond because I want to see exactly how everyone of you feel about this. Trust me, I didn't think it would be like this from the start. But it has felt like meeting your soulmate. Rex has given me the impression that we are not made to have one soulmate. And I feel like he has deserved the privilege to love me as much as I want to be loved. Also, I believe I am ready to love him and pour out the goodness of my heart onto him. It has taken me months to reach this decision. I don't want you to think that I have rushed things. There hasn't been any rush. What we have has blossomed because love, understanding, mutual respect, and commitment have been featured in this relationship.

There was momentary silence in the group after Sophia's message. Her children, it seemed, were dissecting her response.

Sophia reclined against the head of her bed and wiped her eyes. She reread Rex's message, feeling emotional.

A message popped up on the WhatsApp group. It was from Jazmin.

> If this is what you want, then we have to support you. But you have to keep us abreast of your movement. We need to know every detail until we can really trust him.

Sophia nodded and went back to reading Rex's message.

"He thinks I'm from God," she whispered, touched immensely by that line.

CHAPTER 4

The First Meeting

Sophia was nervous as she left her hotel room. The hotel room was Jazmin's idea. She made it clear that Sophia needed a different place to rest, especially if Rex didn't match the character he had portrayed virtually.

Sophia wore a red dress that made her look younger. The dress had a small slit at the back. She wore black pump shoes that matched her black Louis Vuitton bag, which was gifted to her by Jack on her sixty-fourth birthday.

She walked gingerly, clutching her bag against her midriff. The streets of San Angelo spoke the language of conservative romance. The sky was bright and beautiful, and the road had low traffic.

Sophia caught sight of a few middle-aged couples dressed fashionably and holding hands.

According to the map on her phone, The Outback restaurant was a ten-minute walk from the hotel she was lodged in.

Sophia preferred to take a walk because she believed it would help her lose the anxiety that flitted across her stomach.

She loved San Angelo's cool ambiance, and Sophia met a few bars on her walk to the Outback. The bars also looked conservative. Sophia saw a couple dancing to slow music in one bar.

Sophia's palpitation gathered pace once she saw the sign of The Outback restaurant. It was actually a big restaurant. It was a white, storied building with a sprawling parking lot at the side.

Sophia stopped a few yards away from the entrance door and took several deep breaths.

She opened her bag, brought out her phone, and started typing.

I am here

Rex had informed her that he had made reservations in her name. When Sophia walked inside, a host came to her.

"Good evening, Madam," he said.

"Good evening," Sophia responded.

"Do you have a reservation, Ma'am?"

"Yes. Sophia Sanders," she said in a nervous, shaky tone.

"Right this way," the host said, leading her up the stairs to the top floor.

Sophia held the railings and walked slowly. When she reached the top floor, she looked across the tables for a sign of Rex. She couldn't find him.

Only four of the tables on the top floor were occupied, and the couples spoke in low tones.

The attendant led Sophia to an empty table, and as Sophia

dropped down in a chair, she took a deep breath, trying to contain her emotion.

"He is supposed to be here before me," she said in a soft tone.

She opened her bag, brought out her phone, and intended to send Rex a message. She took a glance forward and found Rex in black slacks and a dress shirt. There was a bouquet of pink roses in his hand.

His eyes were filled with excitement and his smile was infused with a quality capable of taming a beast. It tamed Sophia and swept off the anger that was starting to well up inside her.

A frown made way for a faint smile that gradually grew as he drew closer to the table.

Sophia had her eyes on him and could smell his cologne, which appealed greatly to her olfactory senses.

"You are so beautiful," he said, handing the bouquet to her.

Her breath caught in her throat. "Thank you," Sophia said and took a sniff, nodding as she held the bouquet close to her nose.

She looked up at him as he sat in the chair that overlooked her.

The table between them was small and bridged the communication gap between them.

His eyes remained on her, as if memorising her face.

Sophia was still slightly nervous as she kept her face down. She was speechless and racked her mind for a convenient start to a conversation with him.

"I wanted to see you come in. So, I decided to wait outside in my car. You are so beautiful in that red dress and the way you walk. I could smell the dignity and confidence in your stride," Rex complimented.

His confidence and compliment broke the blocks of anxiety that prevented her from expressing herself.

"Thank you. I am still a little nervous," she responded.

"I understand. You must be really tired after a long journey."

"Not really. I am not tired. I guess my desire to see you make every stress tolerable."

"I am so happy to see you. I have thought about this over and over again and...I was desperate to make everything perfect. When you told me you had taken a hotel room, I was mad at myself for not making sure I made reservations for you."

"You didn't have to overthink it. I made reservations two days before. It was my daughter's idea."

"Yeah, but I guess it is just the way I feel about you. I wanted you to be really comfortable."

"I understand. You should know that I think you've made a great first impression," Sophia said, taking a sniff of the bouquet.

Rex fixed his eyes on her hair as she lowered her face. His lips spread apart, and he suddenly looked like a schoolboy in the sixties staring at posters of ladies in bikinis. He was entranced and placed one hand on the table.

Rex took his hand quickly from the table, becoming nervous as he related to the feelings that filled his heart.

When Sophia raised her face up, her green eyes glinted with a wet sheen.

"Thank you so much for the flowers. I really love them."

"You are welcome," Rex said, locking eyes with her.

For a transient moment, they kept their eyes locked together. The excitement and joy that oozed out of them were palpable.

Rex's lips twitched ever so slightly, and a pulse tapped away on Sophia's wrist. "You are so beautiful," he said, breaking the moment of silence between them.

Sophia exuded a blushed smile and loomed her face down slightly. "Thank you," she said in a soft tone.

The waiter came along and stood at the side of the table. Rex picked up the menu and handed it to her. "Order for us," he said.

Sophia read through the menu quickly and went for beef steaks.

"And a bottle of champagne," Rex added.

The waitress nodded and went away.

Sophia dropped the bouquet on the table and took out her phone.

"I have to message my daughter," she said before she started typing on her phone.

I am here, Jazmin. He is sweet.
Exactly what I expected to see.

After sending the message, Sophia quickly dropped her phone in her bag and placed the bag beside the bouquet.

A middle-aged couple came onto the top floor and chose a table at the side. Sophia smiled as the man pulled out a chair, exuding chivalry.

"There is something just peaceful about San Angelo. It is in the air," Sophia said.

"It is a great town. Most of the people here were born here.

So they treat it like their homeland. You'll find that most of them own their houses and try to keep the town peaceful."

"I can see that already."

The waitress returned with their order. Sophia was hungry, but it didn't show in her slow, soundless mastication.

Sophia could feel his eyes on her the entire time. She noticed his undiluted attention on her and tried to avoid making frequent eye contact. Meeting his brown, studious eyes always stirred something in her stomach. There was a rash of goosebumps on her arms already, and her heart was enveloped in ineffable intrigue.

"I have a great schedule for us. There will be a movie night. If you don't mind, we'd go fishing," Rex said, the excitement evident in his bright brown eyes.

"Yes. I have always wanted to try that. I actually fished when I was really young. I went with my father, and I have missed that activity since I stopped."

"You are in good hands then. We will try all the things that you really want to do," Rex said with a steadfast, complaint expression.

Sophia took down her champagne in one gulp, and Rex quickly picked up the bottle.

"More champagne?" he asked.

"Just a little more," she responded, smiling.

He served her glass halfway and served himself.

"You know, when I sent your pictures to my children, one of them thought I was being led astray by your charm," Sophia said.

"My charm? Where is it?" Rex asked, looking over his shoulder. He suddenly feigned a flustered look that impelled Sophia to giggle.

Once she started giggling, a big smile crept up his face. He sat forward, picking up his glass of champagne. He took a short, thoughtful look at it and turned to her.

Sophia had a ponderous look, following the silence in his eyes.

"You know, I have never been so excited about meeting a person. I don't really know how I'd feel if we didn't work out," Rex said, taking a glance at the glass of champagne. "Roger thinks I am overthinking my feelings for you. He thinks I'll find a way to get healing if we don't work out. He is really philosophical and believes the human mind always finds a way to choose itself."

"I would like to meet Roger. I want to see the face behind the advice you've been receiving," Sophia said with a smile.

"Roger is cool and has been a great friend. He has been married a long time now. So, it's hard for him to understand the butterflies that fill my stomach. I love you, Sophia. And I have always had a feeling that meeting physically wouldn't change anything. You've always seemed true to yourself," Rex said, pouring his heart out to her..

Sophia nodded and extended her glass toward his own. She kept hers an inch away from his.

"I was nervous, to be fair. The side talk and experiences of others played a part, to be honest. You know how these talks can make you imagine the worst, but I told my children that this was different. This was beautiful. This has opened my heart and caressed it in all its soft places. I understand it can be scary for them to understand how it feels to be this way, but I am not sure I want it any other way. I want to love you just as intensely. Elli says love makes people become children. Well, I want to be a child. I want to laugh in your ears. I want to talk to you before I sleep. I wouldn't mind listening to bedtime stories from you..." Sophia giggled, taking a deep breath. "After all, children are pure souls. If love makes us pure, then we have to embrace it. We have to worship it like rain in a time of drought," Sophia trilled, her eyes becoming wet.

"To love," she added, stretching her glass forward.

"To love," Rex responded.

They clinked glasses and snuck sips without taking their eyes off each other.

The impulse to resort to tears overwhelmed Sophia, who kept trying to keep herself from succumbing to the promises of a new dawn. Her breathing was harried, and she kept blinking and smiling.

Rex took her hand, dipping his fingers in the spaces between her fingers. He stared deep into her eyes and kissed the back of her palm.

With his forefinger, he caressed the part he had kissed without taking his eyes from her face. Rex's eyes were constricted and unblinkingly fixed on her. The sexiness that oozed out of him as he stared at her sent a love wave across her body.

Sophia struggled to contain the force that carried inside her. Her face was slightly flushed, and as she stared at his lips, the desire to kiss them took over, proceeding like a dictator in a democracy.

Sophia was still reeling from the force of this desire as they walked out of the restaurant. Rex led her to his car and opened the door for her.

Inside, he took her hand and took a moment to look into her eyes.

"Should I take you to a wine bar?" he asked.

"Okay. That'll be great," she responded without taking her eyes off him.

Sophia's eyes expressed unyielding passion with gorgeous servility. The magnitude of the desire that flowed inside her blocked off any lingering strand of reason. She was thinking about him, observing his features like an artist.

Rex loosened his hand from her grip and turned on the ignition. He turned to her, smiling. "It is just a minute drive," he said.

She took his hand, tightening her grip on his wrist as she leaned forward. She had a serious visage, like a patriot singing the national anthem.

Rex understood. The plumes that oozed out of her body had the same smell as the beautiful dreams and yearnings that had left him obsessed.

Hence, Sophia wasn't the only one leaning her face toward him. Rex followed her direction, slowly shifting his face toward her, stitching out an exquisite show of susceptibility.

When they kissed, it was soft, slow, before it became intense and fast. She placed her hands on his shoulder, and his hands settled on her thighs as the sound of kissing prevailed in the car.

When she drew apart from him, she looked better. Sophia had the look of a woman who had just lifted a heavy burden from her heart. Beads of sweat settled on her brow. She looked like a teenager who had just had her first kiss. Her smile broadened.

Rex was hungry for her. The kiss had a different effect on him. His eyes searched her body like a torch in an overgrowth. His lips twitched, propelled by the initial touch of her saliva. The dry feelings inside him could walk again. Rex felt alive. He had the eyes of a man who had just woken up from a coma and marveled at the changes in the world.

"You are...you are...my sunshine," Rex said.

The elliptical nature of his utterance proclaimed the effect of the kiss on him, and Sophia had a better sense of it. It glorified her touch and reminded her of his compliment.

"You are my sunshine," he repeated, clearly, taking a deep breath and wiping off the beads of sweat on his face with his forefinger.

He turned to the road and drove down to the wine bar. He pulled into the parking lot and got out of the car.

Sophia was trying to open the door when she saw him at her side. He opened the door down for her, and his eyes and mind were stuck in praise and worship as she alighted.

He closed the door and closed in on her. He embraced her and placed his head on her shoulder, weaving his hands across her back.

He wanted to be with her, to be close to her, and suck himself into her warm embrace. He wanted to imprint himself in her soul and become a part of her essence.

Sophia weaved her hands across the back of his head as she contended with a noisy respiration. Tears started trickling down from her eyes.

Entwined with Rex, Sophia looked up at the open Texas sky.

Her eyes met the gibbous moon and the constellation of stars in her line of vision. She wondered whether a star was being born at this point in time. A star that was built with the foundation of the love that held them bound.

Rex remained calm as he placed his head on her shoulder. For a moment, it seemed he had fallen asleep in her embrace. He looked like a child.

Sophia was willing to remain in that position with him interminably. There was something about embracing him in a parking lot that left her immersed in a mesmerism she couldn't resist.

Rex drew apart from her and placed his hands on her face. In spite of the little lighting in the parking lot, his eyes searched her face and found security in her visage.

He kissed her lips and looked into her eyes, which remained closed as he drew apart from her.

"You are so beautiful," he said softly.

She opened her eyes. Her expression was solemn.

Rex caressed the tendrils of blonde hair on her brow. He drew a line from her brow to the bridge of her nose and left another kiss on her lips.

He took her hand and led her into the Wine Bar. The wine was tasty and sweet, but Sophia didn't think it matched the sweetness of his lips and the nourishment it brought to her heart.

Fly Me To The Moon by Frank Sinatra blared across the bar. An old couple danced. They could barely move their legs, but their hearts moved, their memories moved, and Sophia enjoyed the spectacle.

"You want to dance?" Rex asked.

"I am not sure I am good at this," Sophia responded, feeling skeptical and shy.

"You just have to embrace me," he responded, taking her hand.

He took her away from the table and started dancing with her. It was a slow dance that featured intense gazes, quivering lips, and deep warmth.

Rex had already exceeded the expectations she had for this date. And it was especially beautiful because their spontaneous moments had expressed exactly what they had in their hearts for each other.

Sophia didn't want the night to end. She didn't want a situation where she would have to kiss him and say goodbye. This was a dance that should last forever.

Later, Rex drove her to her hotel. She wanted to stay with him, to follow him home, and she thought about making it clear to him, but there were other feelings at play at this moment.

He kissed her cheek. "I will come pick you up tomorrow morning," he said.

She nodded. It was the sort of nod that lacked conviction.

As his car pulled away from the hotel, she shivered and felt hot. Her body felt his absence and trembled. Sophia suddenly looked sick and powerless.

Her hand trembled as she took out her phone from her bag. She started typing.

I want to be with you. Come take me.
Come back.

It was the most passionate and vulnerable message she had ever sent, but Sophia felt better after sending it.

Sophia clutched her Louis Vuitton bag and straightened her face toward the direction his car had taken. Her phone was in her other hand, waiting for his reply. The bouquet of pink roses was tucked into the armpit of the hand holding the phone.

Suddenly, she smiled as she remembered the moment she had kissed him outside the Outback restaurant. Sophia looked younger as she stood at the roadside, and the goosebumps on her arms became more pronounced.

Soon, her phone beeped. She quickly took a look at it and found a text from Jazmin. She heaved a heavy sigh.

How's the date going, Mom?

Sophia was typing a reply to Jazmin when Rex's message popped up on her phone screen. She abandoned the message she was typing and read Rex's text.

I am on my way back to your hotel.

Sophia's smile was so bright that her cheeks hurt from smiling. She quickly sent Jazmin a response.

It has been great. It has been really great.

Sophia dropped her phone back in her bag and kept smiling as she kept her eyes on the road. She took several deep breaths.

When Sophia saw Rex's car closing in on her, her palpitation intensified. Her sense of excitement grew beyond manageable borders. She wanted to run toward the car before it stopped.

Sophia couldn't believe the feelings that filled her heart.

Meeting Rex had edited her constitution, infusing qualities that would have come as an assault on her sensibilities.

Rex rushed out of his car and embraced her at the roadside. He kissed her cheek and stroked her hair.

"God. I was missing you so much already," he said.

"I was missing you too," she replied.

Moments later, Sophia was sitting beside him in the passenger's seat. She looked out of the window at her side, caught up in her thoughts.

She was smiling, excited, and exposed to the fact that she hadn't really mingled with this level of excitement for a long time.

She had a great life, and her family was a shining star in the constellation of her life, but contentment, as she discovered, could be monotonous. This was different from her routine exhibitions.

These sorts of feelings weren't supposed to be infused into her everyday activities. She was experiencing the Christmas feelings, and Sophia wanted to be as aware as possible. She wanted to remember every moment.

Rex drove to his ranch and helped Sophia out of the car, displaying the same level of chivalry.

He locked her arm in the crook of his elbow and led her into his home. It was a large bachelor pad, and it was neat in spite of its austere, dull design.

Sophia immediately spotted the modifications needed to give the house the right spark.

He took her to a cluster of three couches curled around a wooden table. "Would you like a glass of wine?" he asked.

Sophia nodded.

Rex picked up the TV remote from the table and turned on the TV.

Sophia barely looked at the TV as Rex proceeded to the kitchen section of his home. She picked up her phone and thumbed through it. There were messages on her family WhatsApp group.

Sophia instantly remembered that she hadn't taken any pictures to show her children. It was in her plans, but the moment with Rex seized her, making it easy to forget these little things.

She took a snapshot of the TV, capturing the table and her feet and posted it on the WhatsApp group.

> Are you in his house, Mom?

Jazmin asked after a beat.

Next, Jack dropped a message.

> I thought you booked a hotel room for her.

> I did, Jack. I think Mom has changed her mind. Or does the hotel room look like this?

Jazmin asked.

> I hope you know it is risky, Mom. This is the first time you have met him. If you can, please tell us how you're feeling,

Sabrina said.

Sophia took a selfie of herself smiling. In the selfie, she stuck out her tongue and placed it at the top of her lip. She captioned it: *I am having one of the best moments of my life.*

Rex returned with two glasses of wine. He sat beside Sophia and handed her a glass.

"Thank you," Sophia said, taking a sip of wine. "It is really nice. Thank you," she added.

"Should we see a movie?" Rex asked.

"Sounds like a great idea," Sophia responded.

Rex stood up, giving Sophia an opportunity to check the responses of her children to her texts.

Jazmin responded with a laughing emoji before she added, *you must really be having fun, but please be careful.*

Jack and Sabrina simply liked the picture without leaving any response. It was easy to think they were still struggling to believe that Sophia, at sixty-five, had found a man who brought an exquisite sparkle to her life.

Rex turned off the lights in his house, infusing a cinematic spectacle. He sat beside her and took her hand as he straightened his eyes on the TV.

Beside him, Sophia had a blushed smile as she remained half-closeted in her mind. She was thinking about the kisses, the clear show of vulnerability, the sweetness of his lips, and internally, she couldn't wait to do more things with him. She couldn't wait to become fully entwined in the constellation of his life. They snuggled on the couch for hours watching tv then they both drifted off to sleep.

The next morning, Rex drove with Sophia to her hotel room and helped her retrieve her belongings.

Afterward, they went fishing. Sophia was particularly thrilled by this activity. Unknown to her, Rex kept taking snapshots of her as she wiggled her line in the stream.

In the evening, they went back to his ranch. Rex's workers were busy with the cows. Rex led her to his stable and helped her onto a white horse. Rex cambered up a brown horse and rode with her across the ranch.

They rode closely together, and this time, Sophia left her phone in his house, preferring to fully yield to any activity with him. The ride around the ranch was quiet, with Sophia taking in all the beauty of it. She was impressed with how Rex had managed to maintain such a large ranch.

"Have you considered other forms of ranching?" she asked, breaking the silence.

"You mean increasing my catalog of life stock?"

"Yes, but I guess specialization is best."

"Well, I already have plans in place to acquire more cattle."

"That sounds like a great idea," she replied softly, smiling.

"Have you ever considered living at a ranch?" Rex asked.

"Yes. I used to as a teenager. In the movies, the ladies who lived on ranches looked really gorgeous. I wanted to be like one. I even had the perfect image of how I'd dress when I started living on a ranch."

"How much have you evolved from that desire?" he questioned.

"Well, reality changes things for us, doesn't it? I mean, I had always lived in the city before I moved to Cabo. I guess that desire got swallowed up eventually."

Rex nodded and became quiet again. They rode across the ranch, watching as the cows were led into their respective barns.

Later, they went back to the house. Rex sent the pictures he took of her in the stream, and Sophia quickly sent them to her family WhatsApp group.

At night, Sophia sat beside the glass wall and took a look at the sky. The sky was beautiful from here. She was drinking from a cup of tea, enthralled by the nature of her vacation.

Rex had a thoughtful look and looked down ever so slightly. Sophia didn't notice because she was fascinated by the pinpoints of stars in the sky.

"The sky is so beautiful," Sophia said, keeping her eyes forward.

By the time she eventually turned toward him, Rex had already straightened his head and sat up. He had a faint smile on his face.

"Are you alright?" she asked.

"Yeah. I am fine. I am a little overwhelmed," he replied.

"Overwhelmed by what?" she asked.

"Everything."

"Are we happening too quickly?"

"No. No. I love every bit of it," Rex responded quickly. "I want things to be even faster."

"How fast?"

"I don't know, but I don't want us to be hurt by speed. You know what they say about slow and steady."

"So, you want us to be faster, but you would prefer us to be slow if it made us steady?"

"Exactly. The most important thing is unifying our dreams and life, isn't it?"

"Yes. How do you feel right now?" Sophia asked.

"I feel really good. I am counting the days."

"What? I just got here. I will be staying for seven days."

"I know, but seven days isn't as long as you think."

"But it is long enough, wouldn't you agree?"

"Not long enough for me. *Eternity* might not be long enough for me."

Sophia exuded a blushed smile and shook her head.

"We'll always have each other. I am actually confident of that. I mean, we spent months just talking and doing things together despite being far apart. That actually takes great work," Sophia said seriously.

"And love," Rex added.

"Yes, and love."

"You want to go out?" Rex asked.

"In the dark?" Sophia asked, slightly puzzled.

"Yeah. We'll hold hands. The night is beautiful," Rex said, standing up.

He took her hand and helped her up from the chair. They went out of the house, holding hands.

Rex kicked a blade of grass like a boy. They walked a measured distance from the house and stopped. They sat down in the field and looked toward the sky. Rex placed one hand on her shoulder, and Sophia leaned toward him.

She pressed her lips together and tried not to dwell too much in her thoughts.

Rex started singing in her ear. He kept his voice soft and melodious. It was *Speechless* by Michael Jackson.

Sophia already knew the song, but hearing it from Rex gave her a different vibe and feeling. It started to feel like she hadn't really comprehended the lyrics of the song until now. She immediately captured the difference between listening to a love song and listening to a love song ministered by the lips of a lover.

Rex took her hand as he started singing the chorus.

"*...When I'm with you, I am lost for words...*"

Sophia looked up at him, her eyes gleaming, her hand caressing his back, her stomach swimming in the nourishing flow inside her.

"Your love is magical," he said, drawing closer to her. She kissed him intently, pushing her body against him and forcing him to fall backward.

Sophia lay on top of him, left a few kisses on his lips, and just cuddled up with him on the grass. They rolled around the grass for a while, but she was back on top of him when they stopped rolling.

His hands were weaved across the nape of her neck, and her legs were wrapped around him. The way she pressed her body against him created the impression that she wanted to be sucked into his body and become an indispensable part of him.

"Thank you so much," she said, kissing his ear. "I love you," she added.

"I love you too."

Roger joined them for dinner the next day. He brought a bottle of wine and a bouquet of tulips for Sophia.

Sophia was slightly surprised when she met him. He was diminutive and lanky. He had dark hair that grayed in some parts, and his eyes were piercing and brown.

He wore a white shirt tucked into black pants, and his smile looked slightly theatrical.

"Thank you," Sophia said, receiving the tulips from him.

Roger nodded and dipped his hands in his pockets. He turned to Rex, who was just standing beside him.

"Roger can be shy as well. I didn't tell you that part about him," Rex said, chuckling.

"You bet," Roger responded, his smile brightening ever so slightly.

"It is nice to finally meet you," Sophia said.

"I feel like I have already met you. Rex kept describing you, and he was right. You are shorter than me," Roger responded.

"Was it an argument?" Sophia asked, turning to Rex.

Rex shrugged and pressed his lips together. "Yeah. He made me place a bet that you'll be shorter than me."

"But that's cheating now, isn't it? He knew already," Sophia insisted.

"Well, I can't blame him. It is my fault. He showed me pictures and videos of you, but I still insisted that I'd be shorter," Roger said, smiling awkwardly.

Sophia didn't know how to respond to Roger's statement. Roger looked up at her and quickly turned to Rex, who had one hand across his mouth.

"Laugh if you want to, dumbass," Roger said, proceeding to the dining table.

Rex broke into uncontrolled laughter, taking his hand from his mouth.

Sophia was slightly surprised by the sound of his laughter. She hadn't seen him laugh so intently. She kept oscillating her gaze between Rex and Roger. Roger was smiling and shaking his head as Rex laughed at him.

When Rex stopped laughing, he drew closer to Sophia, who was standing a yard away from the dining table.

He embraced her, stroking the top of her hair.

"Roger can be quite stubborn. You should have heard him draft out theories about how men were taller than women on average," Rex said.

"But that's the truth. Men are taller than women on average," Roger responded.

"But we weren't talking about men and women, were we?" Rex asked. "We were talking about you and the love of my life."

Sophia exuded a blushed smile after hearing Rex refer to her as the love of his life.

Moments later, they had a dinner of roast beef.

"This is really good. Rex can only dream of preparing a meal like this," Roger said.

"But I made it," Rex responded, chuckling.

Roger had a horrified expression as he turned to Sophia, desperately hoping she would counter Rex's statement. "Did he really make it?" Roger asked.

Sophia nodded, smiling.

"Oh! My God. I won't hear the end of it. Well, what can we say? A broken clock is right twice a day," Roger said, taking a sip of wine.

"How about you just admit I am a great cook? You know it. Why is it so hard for you to compliment me?" Rex asked.

Roger kept his face down, pretending not to hear him. He forked out a piece of beef and took a long look at it.

"Don't try to find any fault, Roger. I know what you're thinking," Rex said, glaring theatrically at him.

Roger shook his head and swooped his face down. He kept his face down for a moment before stuffing the piece of beef into his mouth. He chewed soundlessly and after he swallowed, he turned to Rex.

"A clear conscience fears no accusation," Roger said.

"Your quotes won't save you today. You've finally admitted that I am a great cook," Rex responded.

"How?" Roger asked.

"Are you going to ask that question when we just heard you say it?"

"What do I know? My palate might be a little jaded, you know. In fact, I am starting to get the real taste, and it is not good, Rex," Roger said, winking at Sophia.

Sophia was enjoying the banter between them. She kept oscillating her gaze between their faces, matching their utterances with the expressions on their faces.

"Even you know you sound crazy right now," Rex said and weaved one arm across Sophia's chair.

They remained at the dining table after eating. They talked about politics, San Angelo, and Roger talked about visiting Baja with his wife.

Rex and Sophia accompanied Roger outside when they were done. Roger had a more cheerful, impressed look after he reached his car.

"Thanks for making my friend so happy, Sophia. I have to tell you it is the happiest I have seen him in a long while. Maybe that was why he managed to make a great roast beef," Roger said in a husky voice.

Rex took Sophia's hand as they went back to the house. He had a big smile on his face, luxuriating in his hard-fought triumph over Roger.

Sophia checked her family's WhatsApp group and found

that Sabrina had left throngs of messages on the photos she left on the group.

One particular question caught her attention: *are you thinking of getting married again? You look really happy in these photos. These activities usually happen before a big proposal*.

At her side, Rex was turning off the lights to create a romantic background. Sophia took his hand after he returned to the chair beside her.

He kissed her cheek and turned on the TV. As she held his hand, Sabrina's question kept sifting across her mind. Sophia already knew the answer to her question, but she wondered if it would be coming too quickly. She wondered if it was the kind of fast move that could prevent them from being steady.

"You will love this particular movie. It is called *The Notebook*," Rex said quickly.

CHAPTER 5

Sophia stood at the doorway, her suitcase by her side, feeling the weight of the past week pressing down on her. Rex was just a few feet away, his hands shoved deep into his pockets, eyes fixed on the floor. The silence between them was thick, filled with everything they wanted to say but couldn't find the words for.

She took a deep breath, her heart pounding in her chest. "I can't believe it's already time to go," she said softly, her voice trembling slightly.

Rex looked up, his eyes locking onto hers. "I know," he replied, his voice rough with emotion. "These seven days... they've been everything. I don't want this to end."

Sophia stepped closer, reaching out to take his hand. "Neither do I," she whispered, tears brimming in her eyes.

He squeezed her hand, pulling her into his arms. They stood there, holding each other tightly, as if they could freeze time by sheer will. She buried her face in his chest, inhaling his scent, trying to memorize the way he felt against her.

"I wish you didn't have to," Rex murmured into her hair, his voice cracking slightly.

Sophia pulled back slightly to look up at him, her fingers tracing the lines of his face, trying to commit every detail to memory. "This isn't goodbye," she said, forcing a smile despite the tears. "It's just... until next time."

He nodded, though the sadness in his eyes remained. "I love you, Sophia."

"I love you too," she replied, her voice barely above a whisper. "More than you know."

They kissed, a long, lingering kiss filled with the passion and desperation of lovers who didn't want to part. When they finally pulled away, the tears were flowing freely down both their faces.

"I'll call you as soon as I get home," Sophia said, wiping away a tear. "And every day after that."

Rex managed a small smile. "I'll be waiting."

With one last look, Sophia picked up her suitcase and walked out the door. She didn't look back, afraid that if she did, she'd never be able to leave.

As the taxi pulled away, she watched Rex standing in the doorway, growing smaller and smaller in the distance, until he was just a blur. Sophia felt the ache in her chest deepen, knowing that a piece of her heart would stay behind with him.

Sophia broke down in tears as soon as she entered her home. She dropped down on the floor beside the lounge chair and placed one hand on her face, blubbering like a baby.

She snuffled, pricked by a motley mix of nostalgia, sadness, and love. In truth, she couldn't pinpoint an exact reason for her tears. She was filled with appreciation for Rex's care, confidence in their relationship, but she wanted to be with him, to smell him, to sit on the ranch and look up in the sky.

Sophia lay back, unresponsive to the beeps that erupted from her phone. She was transcended to the moment she was separated from Rex.

Rex was strong. His breathing was raspy, but he was able to put himself together. Sophia noticed his struggle. She was struggling herself, but it appeared she was in denial until she reached her home in Cabo.

She left her bags beside the lounge chair and went into her bedroom, changed, and treated herself to a hot bath. While bathing, Sophia had a moment sitting weirdly on the bathroom floor. She imagined she was on Rex's ranch and looking up at the sky.

Physically, she was in Cabo, but her heart was tied to his ranch and suffused within Rex. She yearned for him, like oxygen, and after taking her bath, Sophia was still reeling from being detached from him.

She felt a weakness in her legs, and her knees kept threatening to buckle under her. Sophia returned to the living room and met messages from her children, Elli, Rex, and some of her friends in Cabo. She had amazing friends in Cabo. They were like family to her.

Everyone who texted her showed concern and interest in her well-being. This realization changed the undulation of her emotions. Sophia started to count her blessings and became thankful.

A smile crept up her face amidst the tears that slowly dribbled down from her eyes. She sat in the lounge chair and took her time to respond to all the messages.

The messages from her children mostly expressed relief. They hadn't seen enough to be confident in Rex's ability to treat her with the finest dedication and love.

When she reached Rex's message, Sophia huffed and puffed. It was a slightly long text, and she knew she was about to be taken through a rollercoaster journey.

My love, my sweetest love. Your smell persists in my house. I can feel you, and I wish it remained so. I know my home shares the same wishes. My ranch has been treated to the presence of a Queen. To the presence of a woman that exudes Godlike splendor. We yearn for you.

Everything is quiet around here. For the first time in a while, we are contending with darkened clouds. Your presence has a face, it has a personality. I miss you so much. I can't get enough of your smell, and I would have to imagine that you are in the chair beside me.

It feels like the light of my ranch has been taken away. What are we going to do with this darkness? I wish thoughts can travel with the speed of light so I can be close to you. So we can shuttle between Cabo and San Angelo without altering our schedule.

> I remember singing that Michael Jackson song. Your love is magical. It has changed my life. It has given worth to the pain that brought me to you. It has given music to the legs of my heart. I feel my heart dancing when I think about you. This is the first day, and I already miss you this much. I wonder how I'd feel after two days, after a week. God! You really are my sunshine. I love you so much.

Tears trickled down from Sophia's eyes as she read his text. There were times she giggled, chuckled, and there were times she marveled at his diction. There were times she wondered how poetry could come so easily to him. How he could think of her and stitch out words that felt like sacrifices for a God.

You are from God, she thought. Sophia remembered those words, and it became increasingly obvious that Rex's perception of her had been strengthened by her visit. There was something about her that filled him like a miracle.

She kept reading his text again and again. It felt like the therapy she needed to cushion the overwhelming emptiness that suddenly engulfed her.

To be loved and missed by him was the truest therapy because it offered the necessary consolation that they were both imbued with the right feelings to eventuate another meeting as soon as possible.

She thought about an adequate response to his message. Her hands were shaking slightly. Sophia screenshot the message, deciding that she was going to frame it and keep it in her living room.

Such impressive compliments deserve to be seen every day. The thought made her smile as she started typing.

I cried. I cried so much as soon as I came home. You don't know what you've done for me with this message, but I am going to frame it. I am going to read it every day. I am going to remind myself that I'm with a man that loves me as much as I love him. Thank you so much. I miss you so much. We are going to have to talk about our future together. I need you every hour, my love.

After she sent the message, Sophia took a deep breath and thumbed down to her gallery. She started checking out the pictures she took in San Angelo. Apart from her pictures, there were pictures of Rex and her, pictures of some of the memories they shared together.

Sophia was nodding, emptying out the plumes of agony in her heart.

In that moment, the sound of the doorbell swept across the house. She looked toward the door, slightly surprised. A text popped up on her phone screen. It was from Elli.

I'm outside your house.

"Wow," Sophia uttered, standing up from the chair with a desperate alacrity.

Sophia hurried to the door and opened it, her eyes dilating as she met Elli outside. Elli was holding a paper bag in one hand.

Sophia hugged her. It was a tight hug that left Elli looking a bit perplexed as she reciprocated the gesture.

"Are you alright?" Elli asked after they separated.

"Yes," Sophia said, leading her inside the house.

"I hope you are hungry because I brought apple pies," Elli said, walking to the dining table. She dropped the paper bag.

She turned to Sophia, taking a studious look at her face.

"Have you been crying?" Elli asked.

"I am okay. I will just get some plates," Sophia said and went to the kitchen.

When Sophia returned, Elli was still mingling with a serious, studious look.

"Why have you been crying?" Elli asked.

"Let's eat. Thanks for the pies."

"Why don't you want to tell me about it?" Elli asked.

Sophia sat down. Elli shook her head and sat beside her.

"Are you being serious right now?" Elli asked.

"I'm actually alright. It's just that I miss him."

"You were with him for seven days."

"Don't act like you don't understand because I know you do."

"You are right. We really should eat."

Elli took a bite from an apple pie and turned to Sophia, who was on her third bite.

"I didn't know you were so hungry," Elli said curiously.

"I couldn't eat today. I didn't really eat much yesterday. I really love him, Elli. I think this is what I've been looking for."

"But you guys have plans to meet again, don't you? Because if you love each other, you'd make plans."

"Of course, we have plans. He is going to come to Cabo, but he has to pick the right timeline."

"Then you need to relax. You look like you're in mourning."

"I mourn his absence."

"Don't sound all poetic on me, Sophia. I understand. I know how you feel, but from what you've said, you are on the right track. Is there something you're afraid of?"

"No. I just miss him."

"Are you sure?"

"What should I be afraid of?"

"I don't know. Maybe he might change his mind?"

"About us?"

"About coming to Cabo to see you?"

"If that is not possible for him, then maybe I can fit in another visit to San Angelo."

"This is your heart speaking, Sophia," Elli said, taking a bite of apple pie. "Going to San Angelo to meet a man you've been chatting online with was a big risk, but you took it. You took it because you wanted to give your feelings a chance. You went to him. Anything could have happened, but you believed."

"Where are you going with this?" Sophia asked.

"I'm trying to make you see that Rex is not taking a big risk to come see you. He shouldn't have an excuse if he really wants your relationship with him to work."

"He has a big ranch, and he works there every day."

"A man in love breaks boundaries. If he doesn't, how can we separate him from the one that isn't in love? These are the things we need to look out for. Some people prefer a love of convenience. A love that doesn't demand so much from them. Those are the kind of people that quit when the going gets tough. I think it is really important for him to keep his promise. And if he doesn't, he has to set another convenient date. You shouldn't try to go to him. You have to make sure you're not dating a man that seeks only his own convenience."

Sophia was touched by Elli's preachment and the serious expression that accompanied it. She could see that Elli was not messing about this time.

Sophia became introspective. There was no doubt in her heart that Rex loved her, but Sophia couldn't dismiss the notion that love can have varying limits.

"I hope you are not thinking about what I just said," Elli chipped in.

"It makes so much sense, Elli. Why shouldn't I think about it?"

"I don't want it to create any doubt inside you. I actually believe that he is going to come. I just want to make sure you're seeing things the right way. The question should always be how far are you two willing to go. It is okay if he doesn't intend to go that far as long as he communicates it with you."

"Rex wants to go really far with me. Look at the text he sent me," Sophia said, handing her phone to Elli.

Elli read through the text, smiling for the most part.

"It is a beautiful text. One of the most beautiful love messages I have read, but action speaks louder. Action is how people build things. Words of affirmation cannot solve most of the puzzles in a relationship."

"You are right. I have no doubt in my mind, but it is healthy to have an open mind. I really enjoyed my time with him. When we talk tonight, I will ask him more serious questions. I really think he is willing to go as far as possible, but there's no harm in knowing for sure," Sophia said thoughtfully.

"That's the right spirit," Elli said, smiling. "I actually missed you. I didn't think I'd miss you so much."

"Why wouldn't you miss me so much? You are my best friend," Sophia said, giggling.

Elli cocked her head one way, giving Sophia a funny look.

"You've become really emotional these days. Rex has finished you with love," Elli said with a theatrical grimace.

"If you were single, I would understand, Elli. Do you think I've forgotten the way you danced with Frank?"

"Oh. Please don't start. That was a one-time thing."

"You are just a baby girl. You are soft, and I know this. You don't have to pretend around me," Sophia responded.

Elli placed one hand on her head and dropped her face comically.

Sophia was slightly nervous as she crept into her bed and drew up the duvet. She took a moment to process her thoughts before reaching out to Rex.

Rex had a distraught, labored look. There were red splotches on his cheeks, and his eyes took on a dampened forlorn look. He tried to smile, but it didn't come out as beautifully as it should.

"Hi, babe," he said, his voice croaky and hoarse.

"Hi, love," she replied in a clear, whispering voice.

A moment of silence followed. Their eyes were connected, but it was easy to see their minds wandering, summoning up questions simultaneously.

In the prevailing silence, Sophia thought about Ellis's observation, but she mostly focused on transforming it into a question form.

"Are you alright now?" he asked.

"I don't know," she replied. "What about you? You don't look so fine," she added.

"I don't think I'm fine. I feel a little cold."

"You think it's a fever?" she asked.

"I don't know. It started as soon as I got home. I think I'm sick because you are not here," he replied.

Elli's observation crept to the fore of her mind. Sophia believed the right moment had come for it.

"I was thinking about a few things," she started, pinning her eyes on him.

"What are you thinking about?" he asked curiously.

"About us. I want to get a few things clear."

"Do you miss me as I miss you?" Rex cut in, dilating his eyes slightly.

"Yes. You know I miss you. I miss you so much, but I want to..."

"Then I shouldn't have to wait for a month to come meet you in Cabo. I can come in a week if it is not too much," Rex said quickly.

His response quelled the thoughts that ran rampant inside her. There was silence in Sophia's mind. There was a smile on her face. A part of her wished Elli could see Rex's face as he waited for her response.

"I was actually thinking about that."

"So, do you think I should come in a week? I can get Roger to look after my ranch. He is retired but wouldn't have to do much. I would ask some of my workers to work overtime. I would hire someone to look over the ranch at night if I can't get Roger to do it."

Sophia was surprised by the ease with which Rex answered her unasked questions. It fascinated her because she didn't think she could have gotten him to give her this sort of response if she had packaged Ellis's observation in strategic questions.

"You really want to come next week?" she asked.

"Yeah. I am serious. I don't want to alter any plans you have in mind. I want it to be convenient for you. In fact, I didn't want to bring it up, but I like to tell you everything. If you feel it is not going to be suitable for you, that's fine by me."

"No. I actually like the idea. I miss you so much. I wouldn't even mind if you were coming tomorrow. That's how much I miss you," Sophia responded.

Another moment of silence followed. Sophia captured the perceptible changes in Rex's expression. The miserable scrims on his face gradually fizzled out, and the shape of his smile exuded a warmth and brightness that followed previous intimations.

The brief conversation sucked out the gloomy aura around them. And as he smiled, appreciative of her willingness to accommodate him, Sophia was smiling as well. She was tickled by his willingness to stretch things beyond the borders of observable limits.

"So, what are we going to do?" Rex asked curiously.

"It would be crazy for you to start making plans to come tomorrow. I think it would make more sense to come in a week," Sophia said.

"A week is more than I expected. I think I can work with that," Rex said thoughtfully.

"Also, I will be able to put the right structure in place before I leave," he added.

"Exactly."

Another moment of silence followed. They locked eyes. Sophia was capturing every nuance of expression on his face.

"How do you feel now?" she asked, breaking the silence.

"I feel serious relief."

"Is there anything bothering you?" she asked.

"It is just a thought."

"Tell me."

Rex heaved a heavy sigh. "I don't want you to take it the wrong way."

"I won't take it the wrong way. I want to hear your intrusive thoughts," Sophia responded quickly.

"What if you change your mind tomorrow? I know we both miss each other a lot, but I have a feeling it is happening because you just left. What if you feel better in two days and prefer to keep our initial plan?"

Sophia nodded and tried to ponder his question, but nothing sensible came to her head.

"No matter how I feel, I won't change my mind because I really want to be with you."

His smile added more color, sifting out an infectious brightness.

"How do you feel now?" she asked.

"I can't wait to see you."

"Elli came over today. She wanted to know how long we would keep doing this."

"Did you tell her forever?" Rex asked.

"Elli would pretend not to understand. She will probably say forever is a long time."

"It is a long time. That is why we are choosing it, right? We want to be together for a long time," Rex responded.

Sophia remained still, almost petrified, as she regarded him. His words, the way they came, and the certainty that oozed out of his eyes felt like the symptoms of an undiscovered madness.

"What are you thinking?" Rex asked, jolting her from her mind.

"I don't even know. I guess I am just...I'm just mesmerized by the way you see us," she responded.

At the end of the call, Sophia kept rolling across her bed. She was excited and scared at the same time. It was true that Rex loved her, but she wondered whether the intensity he utilized was healthy.

What if he stops loving me so much? Would he still care for me? she wondered.

Sophia struggled to assign answers to these questions because the resulting thoughts frightened her.

Hadn't Rex made it clear that he would be with her forever?

Only Sophia couldn't be consoled by this observation because forever was, rationally, not a real timeline. People, young and old, had promised forever and ended up breaking up in a year or two.

As much as Sophia intended to commit to a relationship with Rex, his intensity created the impression that he was mostly responding with his heart.

"But I cannot know for sure. How can I know? Maybe that's how he loves?" Sophia spoke out loud, sitting up in her bed. She reclined against her bed and looked toward the wall.

She had a very solemn look and wondered whether she needed to ask Rex this question. Sophia pondered on it for a while and picked up her phone. She wanted to call him, but she didn't want to disturb his sleep if he was already asleep. She settled for something else.

Goodnight, my love. Sleep well.

After sending the message, she kept her eyes on the phone screen, expecting a response. Unsurprisingly, it came.

My love. Are you struggling to find sleep?

It was the kind of question she needed to initiate another round of FaceTiming.

Rex was lying on his bed, but his eyes were as sharp as could be.

"What are you thinking about? Why can't you sleep?"

"We haven't had any real issue since we started dating. Do you think it is a problem?" Sophia asked.

"A problem? Why should it be a problem? I think we have been able to be like this because we have an effective communication line."

"Yes. That's true. I am wondering if we can cope with some serious problem."

"What kind of serious problem?"

"I don't know, but do you think we'll always choose each other?" Sophia asked.

"I will always choose you unless you do something exceptionally crazy."

"What if you stopped loving me?" Sophia asked, taking a serious look at his face.

"Stopped loving you? Why will I stop loving you?"

"People fall out of love every day. I think there are lots of reasons why that could happen. Maybe you could find someone else."

"Someone else?" Rex asked, shaking his head. "I am not a child. I know there are lots of beautiful women out there in this world, but you are my beautiful woman. I choose you. That's the difference. And I am not the kind of guy who just decides to stop choosing my loved ones. It has to take something really massive, but with you, I know we'd always support each other in tackling a problem."

Sophia didn't know how to feel about Rex's response. It was supposed to be adequate, but life, from her observation, was unpredictable. Sometimes, what was previously not massive could pose a serious problem in the absence of love.

She had a puppy-eyed look as she regarded him. Sophia didn't want to stretch the matter any further. She was already doing too much. Perhaps the vulnerability that came with loving produced overthinking.

"Are you really afraid that I could stop loving you?" Rex asked curiously.

"I really believe in your love for me. There is nothing I want more. I have told my children, and I can sense their concerns. I haven't been in any relationship since the death of my husband. I just want what we have to be perfect."

"I am always going to do my best," Rex promised.

"I believe you. I really do."

"You know, I have thought about this before," Rex said.

"Seriously?"

"Yeah. I have wondered how I'd cope if you decided to listen to your children and decide against continuing in a relationship with me."

"My children have nothing against you. They just want me to be safe. They care."

"Yeah. I know. But it didn't stop me from considering that possibility, did it?"

Sophia was unresponsive, the wheels spinning in her mind.

"But I didn't let it bother me, my love. I told myself that I'm going to love you as much as I can. That way, I'd know I did everything I could," Rex added.

Sophia smiled. It was a beautiful smile that expressed a bit of relief.

"I like the fact that you are already used to the thoughts that bother me. Sometimes I feel like I am looking in a mirror when I talk to you," Sophia responded.

"I feel that way at times as well. I really believe we are going to be alright. If somehow, in the future, things don't turn out as we want, it wouldn't be because I stopped loving you. It wouldn't be because I didn't want to try," Rex added.

"Thank you for understanding my feelings. I feel I can sleep better now. Goodnight, babe," Sophia responded.

"Alright then. Goodnight, my love," Rex concluded. He waved at her and smiled faintly before she ended FaceTime.

Sophia lay on her back, weaving her hands across her stomach. She kept her eyes open and retained a solemn look. She started to think about introducing Rex to her mother and sisters.

Sophia was wary of her sisters and had a feeling that they wouldn't be so keen to trust in the feelings that persisted between Rex and her.

Sophia pulled up her duvet to her neck and lay on her side. Rex's assurance was beautiful, but Sophia understood her thoughts and knew they emanated from a realistic foundation. Nonetheless, she believed she was going to reciprocate his efforts and love him as much as she could.

When she woke up the next day, Sophia found out that her sister, Julia, had left a few messages on the family WhatsApp group. Julia was not constantly on WhatsApp but managed to receive all the messages she had missed out on.

Are these pictures serious? Sophia is dating? Why is anyone not trying to visit her? Nah. I am going to her place tomorrow.

Sophia checked the time of the message and saw that Julia had sent it around twelve-fifteen in the morning.

She heaved a heavy sigh and left the bed, taking her phone along. Julia lived in La Paz, which isn't far from Cabo. She had equally chosen to retire in Mexico.

Sophia was slightly worried about having her in Cabo, and when she checked her message, she discovered that her children had reacted to it, feeding her desire to visit.

After a routine exercise, Sophia decided to prepare pasta and sauce, anticipating Julia's visit.

By ten-fifteen in the morning, Julia sent a text informing Sophia that she would be in Cabo by two pm.

Sophia spent the rest of her morning chatting with Rex and reading a book.

She was sitting in her lounge chair and drinking from a glass of lemonade. After reading for a while, Sophia nodded off.

When Sophia woke up, she was surprised to find that the time was edging past one-thirty in the afternoon. She left the lounge chair and went to her bedroom. She changed into a dress that rustled ever so slightly against the floor.

The doorbell rang while she was in her bedroom. Sophia hurried to the door and found her sister Julia outside.

Julia was wearing white shorts, and she wore a hat, covering her brown hair.

Julia placed her hands on the side of Sophia's face and looked straight into her eyes before giving her a warm embrace.

Sophia staggered backward, moving inside the house with her younger sister.

In the living room, Julia drew apart from Sophia and took another look at her face.

"Are you okay?" Julia asked.

"Yes. I am feeling great."

"Are you sure? Why don't you tell me things anymore?" Julia asked.

"You have a family to worry about. Besides, I am fine. Everything has been going smoothly since the last time I spoke to you."

"Are you sure? Because being in a sudden loving relationship after remaining single for so many years isn't exactly smooth."

"My relationship with Rex isn't sudden, Julia. We have been dating for months."

"For months? And you didn't tell me?" she looked hurt.

"I wanted to take my time. I think I have let it out at the right time," Sophia responded gently.

Julia took a quick, deep breath, taking a studious look at Sophia's face.

"Please join me in the dining. I made pasta," Sophia said, breaking the transitory silence between them.

Julia ate quickly, but Sophia could see that she was worried from the way she moved her fork.

"Seriously, I don't want you to worry about me," Sophia said in a soft voice.

"You know I will be worried, and it's not just me. Everyone is worried. The things I saw on WhatsApp were strange. They didn't look like they were coming from you."

Sophia smiled, shaking her head. "I am experiencing love again. That's the difference," Sophia responded.

Julia took a heavy breath that startled Sophia. She coughed slightly and took two gulps from her glass of water.

"Are you alright?" Sophia asked.

"Yeah. I am fine. I know you are wise, Sophia. I could boast about your intelligence to anyone, but I know what love can do to the mind. There have been so many reports of love scams lately. These people usually target the elderly."

"I know, Julia. I am the same age as Rex. This is not one of those scams. Didn't you see the pictures? I was with him in San Angelo."

"Yeah. I saw them. You know these people bring new updates to scams every day. I just don't want you to be the victim of one."

"It is not a scam, alright. Rex is doing fine."

"He hasn't told you about a debt he needs to pay, right?" Julia asked.

"No."

"Maybe he could call it an investment. Maybe he could..."

"Rex is not like that," Sophia said, raising her voice. "Seriously, Julia. Calm down. You are pissing me off."

Julia was quiet. She dropped her fork and sat back in her chair.

"I am sorry, Sophia. I am really worried about you. Your children are worried as well."

"It is okay to be worried, but you should at least ask me how things are going between us. You think I am stupid? You think I am dumb?" Sophia asked.

"I could never see you that way. But you are doing something really different. Remember the time I encouraged you to start dating again? You told me you see nothing special in the men you've spoken to. What is really special about this one? What changed?"

"His name is Rex, and he appreciates me. He loves me the way I want to be loved, and that's enough for me," Sophia trilled.

Julia interlocked her fingers and started nodding her head as she gave Sophia side-eye.

"Have you thought about your future with him? Does it look good?" Julia asked.

"It is beyond good. I am with a man who desires to love me with all his heart and strength."

Julia's puzzled look became bolder after Sophia's testimony. Somehow, she couldn't make herself believe that Sophia was being sensible, especially as previous intimations suggested that she was hardly pliable to the advances of men.

"So, how do you guys plan to deal with the distance between you?" Julia asked.

"Rex is coming to Cabo next week. That's how much he misses me."

"That's actually good news. At least I'll get to see him."

"I have no doubt that you'd see that he's a good man," Sophia responded.

Julia nodded without any real conviction.

CHAPTER 6

Life In Cabo

October in Cabo was perfect for Rex's arrival. Sophia couldn't help but admire how his light linen shirt and long black trousers accentuated the build and muscularity he had developed from years of working on his ranch.

Her heart felt like it was going to pound out of her chest as she anxiously waited for him. The moment their eyes met as he came through the customs doors, Sophia ran to him and jumped into his arms. They held each other tight, savoring the reunion.

When they arrived back at her condo, Sophia noticed Elli and Julia on her balcony, watching vigilantly as she and Rex walked side by side, his bag in one hand and her smaller handbag in the other. Sophia was smiling cheerfully as Rex whispered something into her ear, making her giggle.

Despite only needing a few steps to get to the balcony, it took them some time because they kept stopping to laugh and whisper to each other. Sophia caught a glimpse of Julia's slightly awkward expression, a mix of confusion and surprise. It was clear that Julia was more focused on her, likely noticing how her joy was so palpable, how her behavior had undeniably changed.

They finally reached the elevator to head up to Sophia's condo, and as the doors opened, they were greeted by Elli and Julia. Rex's eyes met theirs, and Sophia could sense the tension in the air.

"Hello, beautiful ladies," Rex said in a husky, bold tone. Sophia noticed that Elli seemed more open-minded, smiling warmly, while Julia appeared less enthusiastic, exchanging quick glances with Elli as if they weren't sure how to react.

"Welcome, Rex," Elli said, broadening her smile. "I hope your journey was quick and stress-free."

"I was mostly thinking about Sophia," Rex replied, kissing her cheek. "She is worth any stress."

Sophia caught the subtle change in Elli's expression, a mix of excitement and something else, but Julia's reaction was different. If anything, she seemed unimpressed, her response almost cold as she forced a smile and pointed to the door. "Welcome," Julia said, her tone more guarded.

As they walked into the condo, Sophia was aware of Julia trailing behind them, and she wondered what was going through her sister's mind. She noticed Julia lingering by the lounge chair as Rex and she made their way into her bedroom.

"What's up with you?" Elli asked Julia in a whisper, though Sophia couldn't hear Julia's response.

The dining table was set with cochinita pibil, a local dish that had been especially challenging for Sophia to prepare. But the desire to impress Rex had buoyed her efforts. As they sat down, Sophia watched Rex's reaction closely. He had a pleased look as he ate from the ceramic plate, nodding and licking his lips with obvious delight.

Sophia's gaze shifted to Julia, who had a grimace on her face as Rex savored his food. Elli nudged Julia slightly, probably trying to get her to ease up on the grim expression.

"This is really nice. I am not sure I have had anything like this before," Rex said delightedly.

"The local dishes in Baja are a real delight," Julia responded, though Sophia noticed she didn't take her eyes off Rex.

"I can already sense the thrills that bring tourists here," Rex added, turning back to his meal.

Sophia couldn't help but notice how Julia followed the movement of Rex's cutlery with a curious intensity, as if trying to detect something in his mannerisms. But Rex seemed oblivious to Julia's scrutiny, his attention focused on Sophia whenever he looked up from his plate.

Elli's eyes kept darting between Julia and Rex, and Sophia could sense her friend's frustration with Julia's behavior.

"You haven't been to Baja before?" Julia asked, her tone slightly pointed as she glanced down when Rex turned toward her.

"I haven't even been to Mexico before. This is my first time," Rex responded.

"If you haven't been to Mexico before, it would be your first time, wouldn't it?" Julia asked, her remark confusing Rex. Sophia noticed his quick glance at her before he answered.

"Of course," he replied.

"I take it that you don't travel much," Julia continued.

"You're right. Most of my travels have been around the US.

I've been to France once, but that's it," Rex said, taking a gulp of water.

Sophia watched the exchange with a neutral expression, trying not to let her own thoughts show as Julia continued to scrutinize Rex. Her sister's nods were awkward, her gaze piercing, as if she wanted Rex to know exactly what she thought of him.

"Are you alright?" Sophia asked Julia, her tone neutral, though she couldn't help but wonder if Julia had picked up on the subtle tension in her voice. Julia's nods slowed, and her intense gaze softened slightly.

"What's life like at the ranch?" Elli asked, breaking the silence.

"It's great. It's beautiful this time of year and very peaceful," Rex responded, his focus returning to the conversation.

Julia constricted her eyes, sucking in her lips as she cocked her head, analyzing Rex's response.

"Do you have any siblings, brothers, sisters, children? I mean, it takes real loneliness for one to live on a ranch by themselves?" Julia asked.

"I have a son, Allen. He's a fishing and hunting guide. I don't get to see him often because he's always on the road. I have four brothers and one sister. One of my brothers lives in San Angelo, but the others are about two hours away," Rex responded.

Sophia noticed Elli oscillating her eyes between Rex and Julia, clearly sensing the tension that was beginning to build.

Sophia decided to step in. "The fishing is great in San Angelo. There are many lakes within five minutes of the ranch.

The town generally has a different aura, but the men are gentle, and the activities there aren't as chaotic," she said, hoping to steer the conversation away from the uncomfortable topic.

Julia, however, wasn't done. "You know, I am wondering how you guys kicked things off. It's like different worlds colliding," she said softly.

Sophia quickly responded before Rex could speak. "Well, it's not exactly that. I may be more sociable, but we both take our private lives seriously. I think San Angelo offers an opportunity to consolidate that."

Rex added, "Also, I loved her right away. There was just something different about Sophia from the start. The way she talked, the way she looked at me, the way she giggled. Everything about her was beautiful in my eyes. I think when love is in the equation, two worlds can afford to collide, don't you think?" He turned to Julia, waiting for her reaction.

Julia's reply was oddly nonchalant. "I see your point. To be fair, I have heard of so many precariously balanced love lives."

Sophia's gaze shifted to Julia, giving her a calm, neutral look—one that felt like the calm before a storm.

"You think we are precariously balanced?" Rex asked, his tone still light, but Sophia could sense the slight unease in his voice.

Julia seemed to realize the need to tread carefully. "It's just an expression to mean that your relationship is unexpected, considering the distance and everything," she explained, her tone more diplomatic now.

Rex nodded, then turned to Sophia with a smile. "What was the motivation behind this meal?"

Sophia smiled back. "I wanted you to have something you've not had before."

"It's actually great. Is there something you can't prepare?" Rex asked, his tone full of admiration.

Elli joined in, "She's a really good cook, Rancher Rex. I've even tried to convince her to open a restaurant."

Julia interjected with a hint of skepticism. "Did you just call him Rancher Rex?"

Elli grinned. "You don't like the sound of the name?"

"Well, I am a rancher, and I am Rex. I think it's great," Rex responded, his tone playful.

Julia shifted the conversation. "Well, since you live in Texas, it would be easy to visit our mom. She lives in San Antonio. You could also meet our other two sisters."

Sophia exchanged a quick glance with Rex, then nodded slightly. "I haven't told him where Mom lives, alright? I'm sure we'll visit sometime in the future."

Rex smiled at the thought. "I would really like to meet the rest of your family. And December is just perfect, wouldn't you agree?" he asked, turning to Julia.

Julia nodded, her expression softening a bit. "December is perfect, but I won't be able to come. I have commitments here."

Rex chuckled. "Then, I guess we have to make great use of this meeting, Julia, the fierce."

Sophia was surprised to see Julia chuckle. It was unexpected, and it seemed like she had unwittingly lowered her guard. But Julia quickly restored the serious look on her face, as if showing any amusement might weaken her stance.

"Fierce really describes you, Julia," Sophia said with a smile.

Julia shook her head, her expression becoming unreadable again.

Rex seemed to be trying to lighten the mood further. "I think you could consider smiling more often, Julia. A smile looks great on your face."

"Well, I'm the only one you haven't complimented, Rex," Elli cut in, her tone playful.

Rex turned to Sophia with a theatrical, puzzled look. "You haven't been telling Elli what I think of her?"

Sophia laughed softly. "Don't mind her. I tell her everything."

Elli feigned a pout. "She hasn't told me anything. All she talks about is love, love, love. She makes it feel like you're a doctor giving her a prescription of love. One in the morning, one in the afternoon, and two at night. That's all she talks about."

Sophia couldn't help but laugh again, covering her mouth with one hand as she dipped her head slightly. She noticed Julia starting to smile, watching her closely as if gauging how happy she truly was.

Rex, clearly amused, added, "I think you are a great friend, Elli. Sophia tells me about your friendship with her. She tells me a lot about you, and I think you are just gorgeous in the way you deal with her."

Elli, ever playful, teased back, "I hope she doesn't tell you everything."

"I don't know, but I know quite a lot about you," Rex said, smiling broadly.

"I told him about the dance with Frank," Sophia added with a playful grin.

"No, you didn't," Elli responded, her eyes widening as she glanced between Sophia and Rex.

Sophia started laughing again, lowering her face as she picked up a glass of water and took a quick sip.

"Relax, Elli. It's a good thing that you can dance. What's the use of pretending you can't? It doesn't make any difference, does it?" Sophia asked.

"I wish I was a great dancer. There are times I just want to loosen up and hit the floor, but it's actually a very difficult chore. I'm not that confident," Julia chimed in.

"See?" Sophia said, turning to Elli. "Most of us can't even scratch the surface of what you do so easily."

Elli shook her head and sat back in her chair, folding her arms across her stomach. Despite trying to appear angry and betrayed, a bemused look played on her face.

The next morning, Sophia prepared Huevos Rancheros, another local dish that Rex found absolutely delicious. Afterward, she drove him to Medano Beach, where they stopped at a traditional Mexican food restaurant to enjoy some tacos.

Rex was delighted by the distinct flavor of the tacos in Baja. After their meal, they visited the Arches, a famous natural rock formation. Rex was fascinated by the sight and took several snapshots, surprised to find that most of the tourists around them were speaking English.

"Let's take a selfie," he suggested, holding up his phone with the Arches as the backdrop. He was truly captivated by the iconic landmark and snapped several more photos.

"Roger would really love this," he remarked, his voice tinged with awe.

Around two in the afternoon, they drove to San Jose del Cabo, just thirty minutes from Cabo. It was the most developed town in Baja, known for its large squares and historic cathedrals.

"Do you want to see the beauty of the sunset?" Sophia asked.

"Of course."

Sophia took Rex to Sunset Mona Lisa, a restaurant overlooking the bay and the arches. It had once been rated one of the top five restaurants in the world. They ordered appetizers and a bottle of wine as they waited for the sun to set.

Rex kept glancing at his watch, his phone resting on the table, and chewed his food slowly.

"Are you enjoying the appetizers?" Sophia asked.

"Yeah. They're really good," Rex responded.

Moments later, the orange glow of the sunset spread across the bay. Rex tilted his head back, mesmerized. His smile was intoxicating as he raised his phone to take a video.

Sophia indulged him, eager to create as many memories as possible. They took pictures together, capturing the stunning sunset and savoring the moment.

"This is beautiful. I can see why so many people choose to come here," Rex said.

"You haven't seen anything yet. Baja is much more than just the sunset," Sophia replied, kissing his cheek.

They made several videos to share on Facebook and viewed them together as the orange sun gradually dipped into the sea, disappearing behind a canopy of cumulus clouds.

"We didn't see any whales in the bay tonight, but I bet we will when we go deep-sea fishing," Sophia said with a smile.

"Yeah. I can't wait. I think it's possible to have unprecedented fun here every day for a week."

"For two weeks," Sophia added with a wink.

Calming blues music played softly on the stereo as they drove home. Sophia took the wheel, treating Rex to "*Let's Just Kiss and Say Goodbye*" by the Manhattans.

Unsurprisingly, Rex was familiar with the song. He sang along, nodding in time with the rhythm.

"You have a beautiful voice," Sophia complimented.

"Thank you. I used to be in the choir," he responded.

Moments later, "*Killing Me Softly With His Song*" by Roberta Flack filled the car. This time, Rex didn't sing along. Instead, he kept turning toward Sophia, trying to read her expression.

Sophia's thoughts drifted back to Julia's behavior at the dinner table. She wondered what kind of impression she might have left on her other two sisters, Caroline and Jade, and their aged mother. Sophia was especially concerned about their mom, who had been thrust into a chaotic grieving process. The loss of her husband of seventy years and her oldest daughter within six months had left her a roadmap of pain, seemingly impervious to it after all she'd endured.

"What are you thinking about?" Rex asked, his voice gentle.

"Nothing much," Sophia replied, her thoughts still elsewhere.

"You know you can tell me anything, right?" Rex asked, his concern evident.

Sophia turned to him, offering a faint smile. "I know. Did you have a great time today?"

"It was incredible. I haven't had this much fun in a long time," Rex admitted.

On the drive back to Sophia's home, she slowed down as they passed two Spanish-speaking guitarists performing by the roadside. Rex smiled broadly as he listened to them. Even though he didn't understand the lyrics, he couldn't help but enjoy the music. At one point, he began to sing along, hilariously butchering the Spanish language as he tried. He left a fifty-dollar bill in a small box beside them and waved goodbye as they drove off.

Rex started to talk about the band and their devotion to entertaining strangers. "It's crazy how greatness can start so small," he mused.

Sophia simply smiled, not needing to say anything. Rex pulled her into a tight embrace, kissing her cheek. "Thank you so much for today," he said gratefully.

Back at Sophia's condo, they took a bath together. Afterward, Sophia, feeling more vibrant, showed off a few dance moves in the bedroom.

Rex cheered her on, clapping enthusiastically and boosting her confidence. Moments later, they were cuddled up in bed, enjoying a quiet conversation.

"Did Roger agree to look after the ranch?" Sophia asked.

"Yeah. He was more than happy to help out. I think he's been waiting for a chance to do something for me," Rex replied.

"That's really good to hear," Sophia said, her voice soft.

Rex's expression grew more serious. "Why does it feel like something's bothering you?"

"What do you mean?" Sophia asked, her voice tinged with surprise.

"I don't really know, but you seem like you have something on your mind," Rex said, his eyes searching hers.

Sophia hesitated for a moment before responding, "Don't worry about me. I'm fine."

"Are you sure?"

Sophia offered another faint smile. "I'm sure. Let's just enjoy the moment."

Rex nodded, his concern lingering, but he respected her desire to keep things light, for now.

Sophia's stomach started to gurgle, and she felt a bit gassy. Suddenly, there was a pop-like sound. She was mortified and deeply embarrassed that it happened in front of Rex.

Noticing her discomfort, Rex, as always, knew he had to make light of the situation to ease her embarrassment. "Shoot low, sheriff, she's riding a Shetland!" Rex exclaimed with a playful grin.

Sophia's initial shock quickly turned into uncontrollable laughter. She clutched her stomach, tears streaming from her eyes from laughing so hard. Trying to regain her composure, she ended up rolling off the bed and onto the floor. Rex, seeing her fall, laughed even harder, clutching his sides.

"You always know how to make me feel better," Sophia

managed to say between giggles, her face flushed with both laughter and relief.

Rex reached out to help her back onto the bed, still chuckling. "That's what I'm here for," he said warmly. They lay back down, their laughter gradually subsiding, leaving them both feeling lighter and more connected than ever.

Sophia started to smile. She placed one finger on his brow and rolled her finger to the corner of his eye before dragging it toward his nose. Her movement was soft and left him with tickling sensations.

When she reached his lips, she stopped, leaned down, and kissed him.

The look in Rex's eyes was different. He looked like he was thinking about devouring her.

"I love you," she said.

"I love you too," he responded and started kissing her.

It was an intense kiss that successfully relegated the concerns he had about her visage.

They made passionate love for hours, then drifted off to sleep in each other's arms.

The next day, Sophia and Rex went to Sur Beach Club on Medano Beach. Rex was very impressed when they arrived, and the hostess knew Sophia's name and took them straight to a reserved palapa on the beach.

The Fall sky was a lovely blue with patches of white cumulus clouds. They shared several kisses and left mid-afternoon and took a boat ride over to the arches.

Rex was impressed with the sea life. They saw sea lions, whales and dolphins. The boat dropped them off on the beach at the arches called "Lover's Beach."

Sophia insisted he wear shorts and a light shirt over his swimsuit. Hence, it was easy for him to change since he didn't need to carry any bag or demand for privacy.

Sophia handed a bag of sardines she bought from a guy selling them on the beach into Rex's hand.

"What is this it for?" he asked.

"You'll see?" Sophia responded.

Rex held on tightly to his phone and kept taking snapshots.

They walked behind the arches to the beach on the Pacific side and saw a couple of sea lions.

"You can feed them," Sophia said gently.

Rex dipped his hand into the bag, took out some sardines, and fed the sea lions around him. More sea lions ventured toward him, making him a fancied spectacle amongst the unprepared tourists, who hadn't come with any food.

Sophia made videos and took snapshots of Rex with the sea lions. He made funny poses and kept feeding them until he was out of sardines.

"I wish I had more," he said disappointedly.

They walked back to the beach on the bay side because the waves were very rough on the Pacific side.

Rex crept into the ocean and swam around while Sophia made videos of him. He was happy and loved the feel of the water on his body. After making enough videos of him, Sophia dropped her phone on their towels to join him.

Sophia took off her dress, revealing her swimming suit. She joined him as soporific spears of sunshine pervaded the ambiance. They embraced, kissed, and luxuriated in each other's company.

Sophia was more excited in the ocean and didn't look like she was thinking about anything.

"I can stay here all day," Rex joked and giggled, splashing water at her.

She giggled and dove into a wave, swimming behind him and leaving a painless bite on his shoulder.

After they got out of the ocean and dried themselves up, more tourists ventured toward them.

This new batch of tourists came with tour guides, who kept speaking and describing the experience.

"There is another beach a few meters away. You want to see it?" Sophia asked.

"Of course."

When they got there, Rex's eyes dilated slightly as he saw the throngs of people at this beach. It seemed most of the tourists preferred this one. Rex saw a sign that said Snorkel Beach.

"Come," Sophia said, locking her arm in the crook of his elbow.

Sophia took Rex to another part of the beach that had tiny fish swimming around.

"People swim amongst the fishes?" Rex asked.

"No. This is just for your feet. Come on. Try it," she said excitedly as she sat on a rock and placed her feet in the warm water,

The rays of sunset were fading away when Rex and Sophia left the beach.

The ride home was eventful, featuring more calming songs from Sophia's wondrous playlist.

Sophia took the awkward look that slightly bothered Rex, but she smiled from time to time.

They stopped at a restaurant a few meters from her home. In this restaurant, Rex tried oysters and crispy shrimp.

Sophia whispered in his ear, "You know those oysters are an aphrodisiac."

Rex put his hand up and yelled, "Another dozen, please!" They both laughed.

Afterward, Sophia took him to an exquisite bar adorned with flower vases which smelt great.

Rex tried a bottle of beer after a long time. Sophia took two shots of tequila.

The tequila improved her mood and made her clingy. Sophia kept moving her hands around his body, and Rex indulged her.

They tried to dance, but it wasn't so easy for Sophia because the music was faster and required quicker movements.

In any case, Rex eased his way into following the rhythm of the song. Sophia was surprised by the way he moved his feet while still holding on to her.

His stylish movement helped Sophia and increased her confidence. Soon enough, she was replicating his moves.

There were other dancers in the bar. Everyone tried to have fun and catch a break from their monotonous lives.

As the dancing wore on, Rex tried a shot of tequila and nodded, impressed by the taste.

A couple at their side took up more intense moves, jumping up and showing immense strength in catching each other.

Rex had seen this sort of dance on social media, but he hadn't experienced it physically.

Everyone became attentive to the couples, who made terrible

faces, tightening their lips and matching toward each other forcefully.

Unfortunately, one wrong move sent the lady falling and landing on a table.

In spite of the fall, Rex gave them a round of applause, impelling the other observers to join in.

On their way back to the car, there was still dancing in the bar. More people trooped in as they made their way out.

"Is it always like this?" Rex asked.

"That's what you get when you live in a resort town."

"There's definitely no shortage of fun down here," Rex exclaimed, kissing her cheek.

Back at Sophia's condo, they took a shower together and then settled in her bed.

Sophia lay face up in the bed, introspective.

Rex was lying sideways and had eyes on her.

"When are you going to tell me what's really bothering you?" he asked.

Sophia sat up in the bed and reclined against the head of the bed.

"I have been thinking about the day you came in," Sophia said.

"You don't think it was perfect?" Rex asked.

"No. It was perfect, but listening to Julia brought a few thoughts to my head."

"Your sister is fierce, babe. I think she was just being overprotective. I don't really have a problem with that."

"I know you don't. If you had a problem with anything, you'd tell me, right?" Sophia asked.

"Of course I will," Rex replied, sitting up in the bed. "So what are you thinking about?"

"You know how we initially planned for you to come to Cabo in a month?"

"Yeah. You think we should have waited a month?"

"No. I want to be with you, alright. I just feel it makes sense to introduce you to my family. I should have done that when I came to San Angelo."

"We can find time to visit them if that's what you want. I don't think it will be a problem for me."

"It just feels like we just keep moving and moving. Isn't it stressful for you?" she asked.

"Stressful? Come on. I am having fun. Swimming in the ocean, having a taste of these local dishes, how can anyone find these activities stressful?"

"Okay then. It is just that meeting my mom and sisters can get really awkward. I don't think they'll be very entertaining."

"I think I already have an idea from my meeting with Julia. At the end of the day, it is not me that's the problem. The problem is a lack of trust and my sudden entrance into a heart that has known no lover for so many years."

Sophia smiled faintly and became closeted in her thoughts again. Rex drew closer to her, curled his hand around her waist, and kissed her cheek.

"I don't want you to let anything bother you before you let me know about it. Remember, we have to tackle these things together. We have to make sure that every obstacle brings us closer together."

"You are right. I always want to find the right note and

mood. I know we have a great understanding, but I don't want you to feel like we are rushing things."

"I don't really care, babe. I just want us together," Rex remarked.

"Remember your words when I visited San Angelo. You said you want us to be faster, but you will prefer for us to be slower if it keeps us steady."

"Yeah. I remember. The most important thing is that we are together."

"Would we keep traveling to see each other?" Sophia asked.

"No. We talked about this not too long ago, but we didn't reach any real settlement."

"Yes. I think one of us has to move," Sophia whispered.

Rex took a deep breath and placed his other hand on his brow. It was the first time he had shown a bit of anxiety since coming to Cabo.

"I know you love your ranch and all the memories there raising your son..."

"You want me to move to Cabo?"

"Is that something you can do?" Sophia asked.

A brief silence prevailed between them. Rex was thoughtful and started nodding moments later. "I think I can make it work. I would just hire a manager and pay Roger to do a bit of supervision and make sure things are done properly. Also, I could rent out my home. I think I can do it," Rex said.

Sophia was shocked by his response. She didn't think Rex would be willing to let go of his ranch, which he had plans to expand the following year.

Caught up in ineffable joy, she embraced and kissed him. "I can't believe you'd do this for me."

"I told you the most important thing is that we are together."

Sophia nodded and ran one hand across her blonde hair. "I am really happy that you are willing to make this kind of sacrifice for me, but I think it makes more sense for me to move."

"Why?" Rex asked.

"Although I run my real estate business, I don't have to always be physically present. So, I guess I don't have many obligations here. Also, I would be able to satisfy my childhood dreams of becoming a cowgirl."

"Okay, but you got to think about it. I want you to be comfortable."

"I will be. Also, I can visit sometimes. I have made some really amazing friends here, and they are like family to me. We actually call each other our "Cabo Family," but I am sure they'll understand."

"Okay. So, this has been bothering you for some time?" Rex asked.

Sophia smiled, pressing her lips together. "I should have been bolder, but I prefer the slow and steady."

"How about we make it bold and steady?" Rex asked.

"What would be the difference?" Sophia asked.

"You get to tell me anything, especially things that concern our relationship."

"Okay then. Bold and steady sounds great."

Sophia exhaled loudly, looking up at the ceiling.

"When do you want us to meet your Family?" he asked.

"I think I will just go to Texas with you so we can meet them together. Then we can plan a get-together at the ranch with your family so I can meet them."

"That sounds like a great idea."

Sophia drifted toward him, taking his hand. "Thank you," she said, kissing the back of his hand. "Thank you for loving me."

Rex shook his head, almost disappointed by her expression of thanks. "You deserve this, babe. I mean everything I write to you. I love you. I love you so much, and I can't underestimate the sunshine and calm you bring to my life. I have never had this kind of understanding with anyone. You expect me to take it for granted? To not give as much as I am receiving?" Rex asked in a serious tone.

Sophia's face brightened up as she looked into his eyes. She could perceive his love and devotion to her.

When Rex and Sophia arrived outside her mom's residence, Sophia stood on the sidewalk for a while, taking in the memories she had experienced there.

The road was wide and sprawling, but the traffic was low. Sophia placed one hand on her waist and tried to squat. She took a deep breath after she succeeded.

Rex looked a bit weirded out by her display, but he was patient and followed the direction of her gaze.

"This road used to be really tiny. We used to play around here, you know." Sophia said, smiling.

"But two years ago, Caroline called to tell me that my mom was crying. She was sitting in this exact position," Sophia said, pointing to the position she had taken.

"Why did she cry?" Rex asked curiously.

"We had just lost our eldest sister to a heart attack. That experience devastated my mom. It killed something inside her."

"I am so sorry about that," Rex said calmly.

"It is okay. It is in the past now, but I don't think she has fully recovered. Our father died six months before, and she hasn't been the same since then. She has changed and grown disenchanted with life."

Rex drew close to Sophia and placed one hand on her shoulder.

"I see why you are a bit reluctant to go to her," Rex said.

"I don't know how she will take it, but I am sure she'll wish me all the best. But I really want her to be happy. To revel in a dramatic change in my life."

Rex was quiet and just stood beside Sophia, grazing her back and drained in the solemnity that held her bound.

"I am sorry. Let's go inside," she said softly.

They walked toward the house, holding hands. Rex looked around the verandah. It was a small house, but it was neat, and the lawn at the side was neatly cut.

At the door, Sophia knocked once before she opened it.

She saw her mom sitting back on a couch and looking into a book. The knock didn't impel her to look forward at Sophia.

Rex saw that her hair had totally grayed, and her body was very frail.

Sophia took his hand and led him inside, closing the door.

"Mom," Sophia called.

Sophia's voice impelled her to look up from the book. The spectacles weaved across her eyes made them bigger, and when she smiled you could see the love she had for Sophia.

She tried to stand up, but it was difficult, and before she could manage to get up from the couch, Sophia was already close to her. She hugged her and helped her back on the couch.

Sophia could see that Rose had grown incredibly weak. She

was as light as a sack bag, and Sophia managed to stop herself from mourning the cold realization that life took every piece of strength from the aged and weary.

Sophia kissed her cheek and pointed to Rex. "I have started dating again, Mom. I came with him," she said, pointing to Rex.

Rose's expression dampened, and she only managed a glance at Rex before turning back to Sophia.

"Sure?" Rose asked.

"Yes, Mom."

A door at the side opened, and Caroline walked in. She was the middle child of Rose's remaining four children, but she regarded Rex suspiciously, exuding the same look as Julia.

Rex and Caroline locked eyes for a moment before Sophia noticed her.

"Caroline," Sophia called, stretching out her arms.

Sophia walked toward her, closing the distance between them. They hugged. It was tight, warm, and when they separated, Sophia looked at Caroline's cheek.

"You look great," she said, stroking Caroline's blonde hair. She has lost a lot of weight this past year.

"You look great also. Is that the new guy?" Caroline asked.

"Yes. That's my man," Sophia replied, taking Caroline's hand and introducing her to Rex.

Rex took a dignified look and tried to smile amidst the prevailing tension.

Rose was still looking at Rex. There was no hint of a smile on her face, but she didn't look sad as well. It was hard to tell what lurked across her mind.

Caroline made a pot roast and invited them to the dining table. At the dining table, Rose remained quiet. She retained an expressionless look and barely looked toward Rex, who was sitting across from her.

Caroline was the one doing the looking as she sat beside Rose.

They ate quietly, but Sophia seemed nervous as she kept moving her fork in her plate without taking out anything.

Rex took her other hand, dipped his fingers in the spaces between her fingers. Sophia took a deep breath once she felt Rex's hand.

"Julia said you are a rancher," Caroline said in a soft tone.

"Yeah. I am," Rex responded, expecting further questioning from Caroline, but she just dropped her face and continued eating.

"What do you think about him, Mom?" Sophia asked, raising her voice slightly.

Rose looked toward Sophia and took a glimpse at Rex.

"He is handsome," Rose responded and started drinking from a glass of water.

Rex took a deep breath and turned to Sophia, keeping his fingers infused in the spaces between her fingers.

"What is the nature of your relationship?" Caroline asked.

"What do you mean?" Sophia asked.

"Are you guys going to get married?" Caroline asked.

Sophia turned to Rex, confused by the dimension of Caroline's question.

"We have that in our thoughts," Rex responded.

"Hmm. Thoughts," Caroline said, nodding. "Thoughts," she repeated, stressing it this time.

"You know what they say," Rose cut in in a soft, barely audible voice. "It is the thought that counts."

Sophia smiled, nodding. Somehow, she believed Rose's response was a show of approval.

"You are right, Mom. And we hold great thoughts about each other," Sophia responded.

Rose took another look at Rex. This time, she didn't turn away from him quickly. She took her time to look at his face.

Rex tried to smile, but it didn't come out right. He kept making small movements as he tried to empty out the pressure welling up inside him. Rose's rheumy eyes were slightly cold and intense as she kept them on him.

CHAPTER 7

Sophia and Elli went down to Sur Beach Club to lay on the beach and spend some time together. It was going to be Sophia's last day in Cabo before moving to Texas to foster her relationship with Rex.

Elli had spells of sadness while basking in the sun, and there were times she cut a lonely figure, struggling to respond to Sophia's excitement.

In the evening, reality had started to dawn on Sophia. Now it was her turn to cut a lonely figure in a karaoke bar.

Sophia preferred Cosmo shots, while Elli helped herself to shots of tequila.

They sat at their table, looking around the bar, at the dancers, at the cheerleaders, at the croaky voices that took up the mic periodically.

This was an exciting place, but Sophia had become impenetrable as she started to think about abandoning years of friendship and commitment for such a long time.

"Can you really do this?" Elli asked curiously, her eyes narrowing slightly.

"I have already made my bed, Elli. It was the plan I had for the New Year."

"So, this was one of your resolutions?"

"Not really, but I have to do this. It is important for my relationship with Rex."

"I know, but what about your work? What about the real estate business you worked so hard to build?"

"I have sorted that out. I started making preparations for this arrangement in December."

"I know, but I didn't think you would stay away for that long. I thought it was going to be a monthly or quarterly thing."

Sophia paused, looking down at the empty shot glasses perched on the bar top.

"I just have to spend time with him. I'll come down to Cabo occasionally after I've really settled in. If he is going to be my husband, I have to get used to him."

"You guys already look like love birds. But I have to admit that I like what you are doing. You are taking a risk for love.". Elli remarked as she smiled faintly, her eyes starting to glisten.

"Tell me this isn't something you'd do for Frank," Sophia asked.

"I don't know, to be honest. I have always dated the people around me. I honestly don't like long-distance relationships."

"Well, I understand. Dating someone around has its own benefits-"

"That is how it is supposed to be," Elli cut in, sniffling.

"Are you alright?" Sophia stared at her friend intently.

"I am going to miss you. I'm going to miss you so much," Elli responded.

Tears welled up in Sophia's eyes as she watched Elli. Elli dropped her face and slowly wiped her eyes with her middle finger.

Sophia leaned toward her, taking deep breaths as she tried to tighten her resolve. A tear dropped from the corner of Sophia's eye as she placed one hand on Elli's shoulder without uttering a word.

Elli took her time to wipe her eyes. In those moments, the silence persisted between them. When Elli finally raised her face up, she was smiling faintly at Sophia.

Sophia was slightly frightened by the smile on her face. It wasn't deep and didn't show the side of Elli she had grown accustomed to. This was the part Elli had hidden from her in her funny analogies and witty, brazen statements.

"I am happy that you are doing this for your happiness. You deserve to find all the joy in the world.". Elli sniffled as she pressed her lips together.

Sophia wasn't immediately responsive. The emotion that sifted out of Elli's face was enticing, lovely, and ultimately infused Sophia with a mesmerism that she couldn't resist.

"Don't look at me like that," Elli said, trying to find her usual public self.

Only, it was difficult for Elli, who suddenly gave Sophia a half-embrace.

"Are you going to be okay?" Elli asked.

Sophia took a deep breath and didn't know how to answer her question. The truth was that she hoped she was going to be fine. She knew that Rex would try and make her fine, but was that enough? Would that guarantee that her life in San Angelo would be filled with happiness and peace?

"Please, talk to me," Elli urged, her tone filled with concern.

Sophia nodded, but the gleam in her eyes broadened, and Elli saw a few tears roll down from the corners of her eyes.

Elli was speechless and shook her head. "Why are you not saying anything? What are you thinking about?"

"A lot. I will really miss you, Elli," Sophia said, wiping her eyes. "But I didn't think you'd miss me as much as you've shown me. I know you value my friendship, but I have always thought you had other friends that could easily replace me."

Elli shook her head in utter disbelief. "Do you honestly think so? You are my best friend, Sophia. My best friend. There is a reason you are my best friend. You wouldn't be my best friend if you were so dispensable. I know I don't usually talk about my feelings the way that you can, but I have tried to always be a part of your life, to stand by you through every joy and every sorrow."

Sophia's eyes softened, a warm smile spreading across her face as she blinked back emotion. "You have no idea how much that means to me," she whispered. "I really wish you showed me more of this side to you. At least now I have something to replace my memory of watching you dance with Frank."

Elli's eyes glistened with excitement. "I hope you are not going to tell Rex," Elli said.

"I don't know. But I have a feeling I will always find a reason to talk about you.", Sophia giggled.

"There are a lot of other things you can say about me," Elli responded.

"But would anyone be as beautiful as spending time with you and watching you cry?" Sophia asked.

Elli shook her head and waved Sophia off. She picked up the half-drunk shot of tequila on the table and took it down in one gulp.

Elli followed Sophia to her home, and while Sophia was busy in the kitchen, Elli stood before the portrait containing Rex's message after Sophia's departure from San Angelo. Sophia had kept her promise of framing it.

Sophia found Elli standing in front of the frame, her head tilted to one side as she examined it.

"It is really beautiful, isn't it?" Sophia asked.

"It is, but I would easily have forgotten about it if you hadn't framed it. That's what makes it even more beautiful- the way you appreciate it."

Elli joined Sophia at the dining table. They were welcomed by the scent of the fish that Sophia had barbecued, alongside some salad.

"I will miss your cooking. And it's crazy that I'll be reading alone for now. Sharing books and discussing the storyline afterward has been such a huge flex for me," Elli said in a soft tone. She turned to Sophia, sighing deeply. She paused.

"I think I'll miss you more than you'll miss me."

Sophia scoffed. "No way. That is not true. At all. The things you miss about me most can be easily replaced. Hey, you can find another reading buddy."

"Wait- are you saying what you will miss most about me can't be easily replaced?" Elli teased.

"Well, yes. The way you talk. The way you smell. The way you don't take life seriously. The way you confront issues. I don't think I can find that so easily in someone else. I love your presence. I see you as my sister. And you know what? If you were a guy, I probably wouldn't have had to wait so long to meet Rex," Sophia said as her eyes glistened with emotion.

"No way. You wouldn't be able to date me if I were a man," Elli stated.

"Why not?"

"I am nothing like Rex. I am not poetic like he is. I like convenience. I like having people in my safe place. Rex is willing to sacrifice so much for you. You are willing to sacrifice that much for him. You are the female version of him. That's why the level of compatibility between the two of you is unmatched."

"You have a point, Elli. But I didn't say I would have dated your male version because I thought he would be like Rex. Poetry is great, but to sacrifice, one has to be loyal. You're so loyal to me. And when there's loyalty and love, all of the other things can be worked on," Sophia responded.

Elli was touched by Sophia's preachment. Her eyes constricted, and her expression accommodated more emotions. She paused briefly.

"I never saw myself this way. You always know how to make people feel appreciated. And you're getting good at poetry as well. Rex's style is really rubbing off on you."

Sophia laughed. "You know I've always been this way. Rex opened a door that had been closed for so long. I feel like he deserves to walk me through this door, and to hold my hands through any darkness on this path. I don't talk so much about destiny, but maybe some things really are meant to be."

"Poetic." Elli said softly, eating a spoonful of salad.

Sophia started eating quietly again. She leaned forward and

tried not to think too much about indulging a new life in San Angelo.

Once they had finished eating and said their goodbyes, Elli was ready to leave. She had a sad, disconsolate look as Sophia accompanied her to the door.

Sophia didn't look so good. She mingled with a motley mix of feelings that made it difficult to determine exactly how she felt. It seemed she was feeling everything at once. Joy, sadness, triumph, defeat. She was leaving a loyal friend for a loyal lover.

They embraced once again as they walked towards the porch. Sophia felt Ellis's hand tightening behind her. She wanted her to stay, but matters of the heart usually had no commitments to reason.

When they drew apart, there were several wet patches on Elli's face.

Sophia took a quick look at her dress and saw the wetness that Elli's tears had left there.

"Goodnight. Please stay in touch. We can do what we normally do virtually. I can't believe I didn't consider that. We can do almost everything," Elli said quickly.

"You are right. I will keep in touch," Sophia responded.

When she returned to her apartment, Sophia stopped at the door and cried. She leaned her head against the patch of wall beside the door frame and blubbered like a child.

She made her way to the other side of the living room and looked at Rex's framed text. She ran one hand across the glassed surface and reread it again, reminding herself that Rex was the one who believed she was from God.

The thought made her smile, but Sophia wished she could

spend another day with Elli. Perhaps they could venture on a long car ride so she could get used to missing her.

She walked away from the wall and proceeded to her bedroom, where the bags she would be traveling with were already packed and readied for the journey.

She dropped down in her bed and rubbed her hands together.

Will I really be fine in San Angelo? she wondered.

It was the second time she had asked herself this question, but the answers weren't really forthcoming. This wasn't going to be a vacation like her previous visits.

It started her toward the thought that she was asking the wrong question. It wasn't supposed to be a matter of wanting assurances.

Will I try to be fine? I think that's the right question. I think that's how I can keep my head straight.

This new line of thought gave Sophia a better approach to her occupation in San Angelo and in Rex's home. It was the two of them against any limitation and struggle. A true relationship would always come with its battles, but the battles would matter so little if the willingness to fight persisted.

CHAPTER 8

Settling In

The first two months flew past lovingly. There was love in the air, a binding aura that gripped Sophia and eliminated the tiny sense of gloom that threatened to fester inside her.

Rex was perfect in her eyes. The chores were managed amicably. There was always laughter. His jokes were always funny. They ate from the same plate, and stargazing from the ranch offered pleasure on a platter.

On this particular night, Sophia had a craving that had been absent for the past two months. She was thinking about her living room, the lounge chair, the high-laying dining table, the view of the bay, and the smell of Cabo. The smell was particularly important because it spoke the Spanish language and had the presence of Elli.

Sophia's instant feeling was to reach out to Elli. She texted but didn't receive a response after two hours.

Sophia went outside the ranch and searched for Rex. He wasn't there. The employees had no idea where he had gone to.

She returned to the house and couldn't figure out what to do next. She picked up her phone and tried to see whether a response had come from Elli. There was no response.

Sophia would have gone to the kitchen and invested her time and thoughts in preparing a meal, but she had already done that.

She walked around the house appreciating the small redecorations she had made to the house. It had become slightly lively and fresh, but what was she going to do with this liveliness if she was alone in a town where she had no friends?

She wanted to text Rex but decided against it. She was going to wait until six PM. Rex usually came back around that time.

She picked up a book and tried to read. After reading for a while, she was tired. She had read more books in two months than she had managed in a year in Cabo. In San Angelo, books were her way of tackling boredom, but even boredom could be resistant to routine behavior.

Sophia had her eyes on the wall clock and followed the second hand weirdly. She was actually enjoying the movement of the second hand, and for three minutes, she kept at it until it was six in the evening.

She sent a text to Rex: *Where are you?*

She expected a reply in five minutes. Hence, there was no need to wander away from her phone. After ten minutes, there was no reply from Rex.

The claws of boredom thickened inside her, dragging out her memorable experiences in Cabo. The final experience of watching Elli cry featured prominently on her mind. There were other beautiful memories that kept her sane, safe, secure, without a lasting moment of boredom in Cabo.

Twenty minutes later, she was staring at her phone, waiting for Rex's reply. She was hungry but wanted to wait for him. She wanted to eat with him. Dinner was supposed to be around seven in the evening. Sometimes, it stretched toward eight PM.

She took a drink of lemonade. It calmed her nerves, but boredom continued to spread its claws, growing bigger.

In Cabo, she was usually alone in her home, but boredom didn't rear its ugly head and mock the empty spaces around her.

Her face was flushed, and bleary splotches appeared in her eyes. Her phone beeped. She took a glance at the wall clock. The time was edging past seven-thirty PM.

The text was from Elli.

> Oh! Sophia. How are you doing? It's been a long while. I went out with Frank, and he made me promise not to take my phone. We are actually going out again, but leave a reply, I will respond once I return.

Sophia took a deep breath. It was a deep breath that continued for a long time until she started stretching her neck upward. When she exhaled, she didn't feel better. She started typing a reply to Elli.

> I miss Cabo.

Sophia wanted to type more but believed these three words conveyed everything else.

After sending the message, she called Rex. His phone was

switched off. She searched for Roger's number and dialed. The call went through, but there was no answer from the other end.

The time was edging past seven fifty-five in the evening.

Sophia stood up from the chair, squeezing her face and hands. She was on her way to the kitchen when it dawned on her that something could have happened to both Rex and Roger.

This thought sent a shiver up her spine, and a weakness, a terrible weakness, stabbed her knees. Sophia leaned against the wall quickly because she feared she would fall down as her knees kept buckling from the fright that engulfed her.

She was breathing heavily, unwilling to imagine the worst, but the worst kept creeping up on her, like a prey stalking a predator.

She didn't have to think about feeling the effects of her fear, but as she pulled away from the wall, willing to reach out to Allen, Rex's son, she heard the sound of Rex's truck.

The sound crippled every trace of fear inside her, but it brought anger, overwhelming anger that Sophia tried to talk out of her head.

It was difficult. Rex shouldn't be returning at this time.

"Where were you?" she asked, confronting him at the door, partly out of breath from all of the pacing.

"I am so sorry," he replied, the smell of whiskey wafted out of his breath. Sophia's expression grew even more weary. She had been worried sick. Her stomach churned.

"Why are you sorry? What have you done?", she said softly.

"I should have called and informed you that I wouldn't be returning early." His hand reached out, brushing her cheek, while his gaze struggled to focus, wavering between earnestness and a tipsy haze.

"What were you doing?". She looked up at him.

"I had to attend a friend's retirement party. We stopped by for one drink, but they wouldn't let us leave once we got there.", he continued.

"Who's we?" Sophia's eyebrows furrowed.

"Roger and I," he stated blankly.

"Why was your phone switched off?"

"My battery died. I would have reached you with Roger's phone, but he forgot it at home."

Rex's explanation made sense, but Sophia was still angry. Her face was squeezed, and she started to wonder whether Rex was lying.

"When did you know you would be attending the party?" she asked.

Rex drew close to her and dropped his hands on her shoulder. She pulled away from him.

"I actually forgot. It was Roger that reminded me."

"Are you telling me the truth?" Sophia asked, checking out his eyes.

"I am." Rex drew closer to her and placed both hands on her shoulder. "Were you worried?" he asked.

She turned away from him and went to the kitchen, serving dinner and fighting off the anger that continued to linger inside her.

Sophia felt like crying. She realized that the anger was not just because of what Rex had done. Cabo was calling, and a part of her wanted to answer its call.

Dinner was eaten quietly. Sophia was containing the anger inside her and preferred not to speak. She could still smell the whiskey from Rex's breath.

She wanted to confront him about it. She wanted to ask him why he decided to drink that much when he was aware that he would be driving.

Rex kept turning toward her. He kept looking into her face, but she didn't want to look back at him. She started to remember other little things that Rex hadn't done in the past.

The little things were magnified by the anger that lingered inside her. The anger had a voice, and it spoke resentment into her head, reminding her that she deserved better. Anger brought back flashes of her happy memories as a single woman.

"Remember what we talked about, Babe," Rex said in a calm voice. "Bold and steady. That's how we can win the race."

His voice was lightning. It struck the anger inside her, incapacitating it.

Sophia remembered the promises of love, care, and communication, and she felt a bit bad about the way her thoughts kept getting worse until now.

"Next time, maybe I should go with you if you want to go to these parties. You know I don't have friends here. I get lonely sometimes, and I miss Cabo." She let out a quiet sigh.

"You're right, Babe. I'm sorry. It won't happen this way again." He sounded sincere.

"I also don't want you drinking too much when you go out." She looked into his eyes intently.

"I understand. I didn't really drink too much. I only had a couple. Roger actually spilled his drink on me."

Sophia nodded. The anger inside her had died, but it wasn't exactly replaced with joy. It was replaced with worrying droplets of indifference until he stood up and took her hand, helping her up from her chair.

He placed his hands on her shoulder and kissed her forehead. Now she felt something different in her stomach.

"I love you," he said in a sibilant tone. His eyes were unblinkingly placed on her.

"I love you too," she responded, but her words lacked conviction.

Sophia believed she needed time. She needed to sleep on it. She needed to find a way to tackle this sudden rush of homesickness.

"Let's go out for a walk," Rex said and took her hand, leading her outside the house.

They held hands and quietly walked two hundred yards around the ranch.

His silence was effective in making her focus on the things that mattered. She thought about the sacrifices that she had made, but she still found herself worrying about the sacrifices that she would have to keep making.

"I'm sorry I haven't been able to help you stop missing Cabo. I was only there for a week, and I miss the place too. I mean, it has everything a person would want. I understand how you feel."

"It is not your fault." She smiled at him faintly.

"I know, but you made this sacrifice for me, and I really appreciate it." He stopped in his tracks to take both of her hands in his.

"You would have done the same for me," she responded.

Rex took a deep breath and drew closer to her, weaving his arms around her shoulders. "I know how homesickness can fester. I know how it can make you feel like you've made the wrong choice." He paused. "Sophia, I will always be here to listen, and to talk you out of these terrible feelings. We can work on making your life and your commitments secure. I know working as a broker from here is not easy. I just want you to know that I don't take your sacrifices for granted."

Sophia's expression was different now. Rex had his way with words. His actions were beautiful, but his words always showcased his incredible level of awareness.

"I'm not sure if I would have been able to keep up if I wasn't doing this with you," Sophia said softly. "I don't know why I miss Cabo so much all of a sudden."

He smiled softly as he cupped her face with one hand and raised her chin with his fingers of the other hand. She looked up at him, and her heart beat a little faster.

"You're getting used to me. And that, my love, can be a problem. The person who said familiarity breeds contempt knew exactly what they were saying. I think the real test starts now. When you were lonely in Cabo, you got used to it. I am sure it took time, but you knew you had to, and you also tried to do the things that would make you secure with your own company. I think you might need to start thinking in that direction again. I think it would help if you did that. Once you find security here, it won't matter if you're in San Angelo or Cabo."

Sophia took another deep breath and looked up at the sky. She caught sight of a shooting star, but it was too fast to draw Rex's attention to it. It was too fast to make a wish.

"I think you're right. I will try. I will keep trying."

"Bold and steady," Rex said, kissing her cheek. He took her hand, wrapping his hand around her wrist. "Let's go back inside."

Sophia nodded and went inside with him, grateful that she

hadn't let her anger take control of her response toward him.

CHAPTER 9

Proposal And Engagement

This night was different. It was supposed to start with dinner and end with a movie in the living room, but Sophia was wearing a beautiful purple dress. Rex had insisted on it. He wanted to take her out on a date. And the smile on his face, the energy that brimmed through his body, indicated that something was brewing in the offing.

Rex wore a gray jacket and black pants. He went with a corporate, business look. It was different from what he usually wore. He looked like he could be on TV telling people about the fiscal crises.

He helped her inside the car, and while they were inside, he stretched toward the backseat and brought out a bouquet of red roses. He handed the bouquet to her, giving off a smile that didn't particularly help Sophia's curious mind, which had descended into an inordinate rampage.

"What are you up to?" she asked, sniffing the bouquet without taking her eyes off him.

"I am trying to make today as beautiful as possible," he said grinning.

"Why today? What's special about today?" Sophia asked.

"I don't know, but I feel I should make it beautiful," he responded and turned on the ignition.

Music wafted up from the stereo. Sophia sat back beside him, sniffing the roses and taking frequent looks at Rex, who mostly kept his eyes on the road.

Rex stopped at the Peasant Village Restaurant and helped Sophia out of the car. He took her hand as she held the bouquet with her other hand.

Rex's eyes exuded an intense, loving gaze. His lips twitched, giving off qualities that reminded Sophia of their first date at Outback.

They sat at a table, drank from their respective glasses of wine. It was a beautiful date, but Sophia's mind was not settled. The timing of the date didn't follow their usual planned, thoughtful route.

Spontaneity left room for curiosity, expectation, and Sophia's mind mingled with interpenetrating thoughts that made the entire introspective process difficult.

"What are you up to, Rex?" Sophia shifted in her seat slightly.

"Up to?" He grinned again. He had that same charming smile as he did back then.

"Have you done something? You made a mistake that would get me angry? Is this your way of apologizing?"

Rex drew back from the table, abandoning his glass of wine. He folded his hands across his stomach, giving her a puzzled look. "Why don't you just relax and enjoy the moment?" Rex asked.

Sophia froze for a minute. Why had she been feeling so uneasy around him? Why couldn't she trust him? Why was she missing Cabo so much? Why couldn't she enjoy that he was trying so hard to make her happy?

"I am trying, alright. But it is not so easy. You can't sneak up on me like that and not expect me to wonder."

"I want you to wonder, but think about love, about sunshine, about us."

"Well, I am thinking about us," Sophia responded thoughtfully.

Rex nodded, adjusting forward. He picked up the glass of wine and took another sip. It was followed by another quick sip that left touches of red wine on his lips. The smear left his lips red and sexy. His tongue ran across his bottom lip.

Sophia felt a sudden rush of heat run through her. She stopped trying to determine the essence of the date and thought about kissing his lips while they were freshly smeared with wine.

"Want to dance?" he asked, staring into the jade of her eyes.

"Yes." She replied without pause. Her heart was pounding against her chest.

He took her hand and pulled her close. She left a quick kiss on his lips, tasting the wine on them.

It was a slow dance. Sophia barely moved her feet, and her eyes were thoroughly fixed on him. He was equally looking at her, whispering sweet words as they danced.

Sophia started to smile as they danced on. She was more relaxed and immersed in the beauty that sifted out of having Rex close.

She reckoned she would never tire from being huddled up with him in a romantic dance.

He embraced her, pulling her close and weaving his arms around her back.

Rex left kisses on her neck and smiled faintly as she shivered from the touch of his lips on her neck.

At the end of the date, Rex led her into the car and drove back home.

Sophia sniffed the bouquet on the way home, trying to think about Rex's sudden decision to take her to the Peasant Village. Nonetheless, she loved it and believed that such spontaneous gestures would only bring them closer together.

Sophia dropped down in a chair and watched Rex proceed to the kitchen section of their home.

She peered across the room trailing his movements as he swiftly made his way around. He returned with two glasses of wine. He handed a glass to Sophia and sat beside her.

She nodded, thankfully, and took a sip of wine, taking a deep breath afterward.

"Thank you for sticking with me," Rex smiled softly.

Sophia smiled and turned to him. "It hasn't been so difficult, to be honest. I think I should thank you."

"You made sacrifices that were difficult. I don't take that for granted. I should be the one thanking you." He smiled.

"You don't have to thank me." Sophia looked up at him.

"Even when you're lonely, you stick with me and bring your best self whenever you speak to me." He continued. He took her hand and stood up, helping her up.

Sophia stood up and watched as Rex suddenly remained motionless as if in deep thought.

"What are you thinking about?" Sophia asked.

"You," he said in a tiny voice. "Come with me," he said, leading her outside the ranch.

Sophia was tired, but being with Rex invigorated her.

As much as she loved him, Sophia was slightly concerned about the way he went about his day. She didn't know whether he was feeling sadness or intense love. She didn't know whether Rex had awful news up his sleeve.

They walked around the field as Sophia contended with a slight dose of anxiety. She stopped suddenly and turned to him.

"If there is something bothering you, you'd tell me, right?" she asked.

"Yeah. Of course." He continued staring at the pavement as he replied.

"You will tell me no matter the issue?" She didn't know what she was expecting to hear from him.

"Yeah." He repeated fidgeting with his sleeve.

"Are you sure?" Sophia wasn't sure.

"Yeah." This time he looked directly at her.

"Is something bothering you?" she finally asked.

"No." He replied.

She looked into his eyes even though she couldn't see his face clearly in the field.

Sophia turned away from him and looked into the night sky, luxuriating in the pinpoint of stars overhead.

She took a step away from Rex, taking deep breaths.

"It is so beautiful," she commented, wishing she could touch the sky and the gibbous moon overhead. "Rex, look."

Sophia turned back and found Rex on one knee. He was

holding out a ring in a small red box. She couldn't believe what she was seeing.

Is this real? Is this happening?

"Will you marry me?" Rex whispered, holding his heart out on his sleeve.

Sophia was shocked by this gesture. She felt her heart leaping out of her chest and took a few steps backward, shaking as she looked toward him.

Quickly, she ran one hand across her face, succumbing to deep breaths as if she were close to passing out.

It was easy to think she was dreaming. And wouldn't it just be convenient for Rex to propose on the spot where they had watched the open Texas sky on her first visit to San Angelo?

"Rex- is this a dream?" she said, taking a deep breath.

"I love you, Sophia. I love you with all of my heart. I have loved you since the day that I met you." Rex said shakily.

"Rex I can't believe it!" she repeated, tears dribbling down her face.

Sophia was still shaking, drained in disbelief. She took a step forward and felt heavier than ever.

"I couldn't think of anything I want more than spending the rest of my life with you. You are the one person I couldn't live without," Rex said, impelling her to take further steps forward until she was standing very close to him.

Sophia's hand was shaking as she stretched it forward. More tears started to trickle down her face as Rex placed the ring slowly on her fourth finger.

Sophia helped Rex up and embraced him.

"Yes, Rex. Yes. I love you. I love you so much," she giggled.

Sophia was standing outside her mom's home in San Antonio and staring at the ring on her finger. She hadn't broken the news to her children yet.

Stretching her ring finger forward, Sophia attempted to take a snapshot of the ring.

As she steadied the camera, Rose walked out of the house, limping ever so slightly as she made her way onto the background of Sophia's picture.

Sophia took the snapshot and immediately felt it was the best picture she had taken in a long time.

She fixed her eyes on it, delighted by the way it captured Rose, whose mouth was slightly open as she tried to call Sophia's name.

Caroline joined Rose on the porch, took her hand, and gave her a tired look.

"I told you not to go out until you take your medicine," Caroline said sharply, furrowing her eyebrows in frustration.

"I want to see Sophia. I want to touch her," Rose responded.

There were obvious tinges of desperation in her tone.

Sophia embraced Rose, who showed more affection toward her than the last time she came with Rex.

Rose wouldn't take her hands from behind Sophia.

"I have missed you so much," Rose said slowly.

Sophia led her into the living room and watched as Rose took her medicine.

After she finished taking her medicine, Sophia posted the picture she had taken on the family's WhatsApp group.

"I am tired of these meds. I am tired of the pain. I have suffered so much, Sophia," Rose stated as her voice trailed off towards the end.

Sophia shifted toward Rose and allowed her to lean her head against her shoulder.

"You will be fine, Mom," Sophia said, caressing her back.

"You know that's not true. I am broken. Maybe in another life, I'll be fine," Rose responded.

Sophia was concerned by Rose's tone. She looked over her shoulder and toward the dining table in search of Caroline. She was not there.

"You have always wanted us to be happy, Mom. I think we are happy. Your children are happy." Sophia tucked a strand of hair behind her ear.

"Yes. I am proud of you. I am proud of your sisters. I am happy for you guys." Rose smiled.

"I wish you could let go of the past, Mom", Sophia continued.

"I wish the same, Sophia. But the losses never go away. The memories stay with you, and some of us are not as strong as you," Rose responded.

"You are strong, Mom. I learned strength from you," Sophia said, stretching her engagement ring toward her.

"I got engaged, Mom. Love has really given me another chance."

Rose smiled. It was a broad, big smile, and Sophia instantly wished Rose would keep that smile on her face interminably.

Rose took her ring finger and inspected the ring while keeping a big smile on her face.

"It is beautiful. It is very beautiful," Rose said, raising the ring toward her face. She kissed it.

"You are blessed, Sophia. Your relationship is blessed," she said.

Sophia nodded, sniffling as tears welled up in her eyes.

"I don't really know Rex. But I can see you love him so much," Rose said, caressing the ring ever so slightly.

"Yes, Mom. I love him so much. And he has treated me with the utmost love and care."

"Love is beautiful, but marriage is all about compromises. I'm sure you already know that."

"I know, Mom," Sophia said, embracing Rose.

Sophia heard a knock at the door. She got up to answer it, and the door opened, revealing her older sister Jade. She was elated to see her. They gave each other a big hug and then proceeded back to the living room with Rose.

"I didn't know you were coming over," Sophia said to Jade.

"Well, I saw your post on the family's WhatsApp group and had to come over and congratulate you on your engagement," Jade replied.

"Are you for real?" Caroline asked, hurrying toward the living room.

She had a shocked look and kept looking at her phone screen.

"This really happened?" Caroline asked, showing Sophia the picture she had posted in the family's WhatsApp group.

"Yes. Rex proposed," Sophia responded with a smile.

"He is really serious. He really loves you," Caroline said, looming her face down slightly.

"You thought he was joking?" Sophia asked.

"I didn't know what to think, to be honest, but I was afraid things would get messy if it ended badly. You really took a risk, and I was hoping it would pay off," Caroline responded.

"I understand," Sophia said, picking up her phone and checking out the WhatsApp group.

There were messages from her children and Julia. Sabrina was especially shocked that Rex had proposed to Sophia.

Jazmin left a comforting message.

> This is beautiful, Mom. You should have seen the way I screamed as soon as I saw your picture. Love is beautiful and I'll always be cheering for you.

"It is a diamond ring?" Caroline asked, inspecting Sophia's finger.

"Of course it is, Caroline," Sophia replied.

Caroline was deafened by Sophia's response. She dropped down on the handle of the chair beside her and took her ring finger, inspecting the ring. Jade and Caroline both admired the ring in amazement at how beautiful it was.

"This is so beautiful Sophia. How could you say no to such a beautiful ring," Caroline joked, giggling. "I am happy for you," she added.

TODAY WAS BEAUTIFUL, LIKE THE OTHER DAYS AFTER

Rex's proposal. It had been two months since the proposal, but it felt like it had only happened a week ago.

Sophia was in a boutique called Sassy Fox, getting measured for her wedding dress. She had already decided on the style after seeking Rex's opinion and preference.

Rex and Sophia were sitting on the couch, wedding magazines spread out before them.

"You know," Rex began, flipping through one of the magazines, "I've been thinking about the tux. I was leaning towards a white one. I've never worn a white tux before, and it might be nice to try something different for the wedding."

Sophia looked up from her notes, a small smile playing on her lips. "I get that, Rex, but white? It's not really your style. You've always looked amazing in black. Plus, black is timeless. You'd look so sharp in a black tux, and it's a classic look that you know works for you."

Rex raised an eyebrow, considering her words. "Yeah, but isn't this the time to try something new? It's our wedding—shouldn't I step out of my comfort zone a little?"

Sophia leaned closer, her expression softening. "I see where you're coming from, but think about it. This isn't just any day. It's *the* day. You should feel like the best version of yourself, not like you're experimenting with something you're unsure about. Besides, you know how much I love seeing you in black. It's your best color."

Rex chuckled, setting the magazine aside. "You always know how to make a convincing argument. You really think black's the way to go?"

Sophia nodded, her eyes sparkling. "I do. But ultimately, it's your choice. I just want you to feel confident and comfortable.

And, selfishly, I want to be able to look at our wedding photos and see you in a tux that makes you look as amazing as I know you are."

Rex grinned, giving in with a playful sigh. "Alright, alright. Black it is. You've convinced me. But," he added with a teasing smile, "you owe me a dance at the reception for this compromise."

Sophia laughed, leaning in to give him a quick kiss. "Deal. And I promise, you'll look incredible in that black tux. We're going to make this day perfect, together."

Rex smiled, feeling the warmth of her words settle in his chest. "I know we will. And you know what? I think I'm starting to like the idea of a black tux more already."

"Good," Sophia said, her voice softening. "Because I can't wait to see you in it, standing at the altar, waiting for me."

Rex took her hand, squeezing it gently. "And I can't wait to see you walking down the aisle, making everything worth it."

After having her measurements taken, Sophia joined Rex in the car outside.

They drove back to the ranch, singing *My Way* by Frank Sinatra together.

Back in the house, Sophia sat in the chair close to the glass wall and just looked forward, reminiscing. She had a faint smile on her face as her mind wandered to the very first time she matched Rex on Over50.

She was experiencing life the way she had envisaged, and in this moment, a sneaky thought crept into her mind. Sophia tried to avoid this thought because it was negative.

Only, sometimes, in a room filled with positive thoughts, the tiniest bit of negativity shone brightly and sought to be noticed.

If everything was going as planned, wouldn't it be sensible to think that something horrible lurked in the offing?

Sophia accommodated this thought and rejected it. She wanted to believe that goodness, delight, and love would continue to follow her. She wanted to believe that she had become detached from a world where people expected negativity amidst a sustained rush of happiness and positivity.

Sophia was solemn, but it wasn't exactly easy to relegate this thought back to the abyss it had ventured out from. If anything, a warm flush swept through her stomach. Internally, her body embraced this energy despite her best attempts to resist it.

As soon as she noticed her body's unusual response, Sophia jerked herself from her mind. She decided that she needed to invest her energy in something else.

She tried reading a book. She picked a collection of short stories by Stephen King. Sophia tried to read a particular short story called *The Body*.

However, the first paragraph of the book drew her back to the horrors she was running away from.

She dropped the book and looked up at the ceiling.

Count your blessings, her mind's voice whispered.

Sophia tried to focus on her accomplishments, raising a healthy, beautiful family. Finding love in the hands of the rarest kind of lover.

She started to feel better. It started to feel like she had succeeded in pushing the negative thoughts away.

Only, amidst the blessings that permeated her mind, Sophia had a feeling that the negative thoughts would come rushing in once she tried to relax.

She wondered whether she could instead try to let herself be.

She started to think that negative thoughts were normal as long as they didn't affect the trajectory of her life.

She remembered the time she had thought about death after the unfortunate death of her husband. At the time, she was afraid that she could die and make life difficult for her children.

This fear stayed with her for a long time. It made her careful and cautious of the moves she made in her everyday life.

Perhaps this current negative energy shared the same nature as the one that tormented her after her husband's death. Perhaps it was just another form of warning.

Rationalizing this fresh rush of fear made her better. It strengthened her. Also, she saw Rex having a conversation with an employee at the ranch and started to smile.

Rex looked toward the glass wall even though he couldn't see her from outside. He waved.

Sophia stood up from the chair and went to the kitchen. She leaned against the kitchen sink and weaved her arms across her stomach.

In that moment, Cabo came to her mind. Her home, the lounge chair, flashed before her eyes like lightning.

She pulled away from the kitchen, reeling forward as nostalgia twisted around her like a snake.

Sophia had a vivid image of Elli speaking, the way she moved her lips, the way her eyes shone excitedly, and the way she played down the beauty of love.

She went to bed and tried to rest. She had been busy and wondered whether this rush of feelings emanated from stress.

She fell face down in the bed and splayed her arms apart, closing her eyes.

Sophia felt better in this position. She felt sleepy and could feel the start of a slow rush of nourishment.

Sophia was nodding off when her phone beeped. It was not a loud beep, but because she was expectant, the sound of the beep unnerved her. When she opened her eyes, her heart was beating fast, and a sticky rush flitted across her stomach.

She stood up from the bed, feeling a weakness in her knees. It felt like a strange aura prevailed across the house and weaved itself around her.

Sophia could feel something, but she couldn't place her hand on it. Yet, she had the feeling that she might have a clearer picture if she picked up her phone and checked the message she had just received.

The importance she placed on this message made it even more difficult to pick up her phone when she reached the table. Her hand was shaking. Her knees were shaking.

Suddenly, she took a long, deep breath. In that moment, Rex walked inside the house.

"Are you alright, baby?" he asked.

Sophia didn't turn toward him. She was unresponsive but became more inclined to pick up her phone. Once she picked it up and looked at it. She found that the message was from Caroline.

Sophia thumbed on it, read through it, and staggered backward. Her phone slipped from her hand as her breathing became raspy.

"Are you okay?" Rex asked, running toward her and placing one hand on her shoulder.

Sophia might have collapsed on the floor if she hadn't gotten that support from him. Her body had become pale, and there were perceivable scrims of darkness in her eyes.

"What's the problem?" Rex asked.

Her knees buckled under her, but Rex showed immense strength in holding on tightly to her.

He pulled her toward a chair and helped her down. There was panic in his eyes, and a pulse tapped away on his wrist. He was fraught with fright and started checking her pulse.

Sophia was fine, but she was dealing with something different, something dark, and Rex sensed it.

He caressed her back and neck.

"Should I take you to the bed?" he asked, confused.

Sophia remained unresponsive and just looked forward, confused, as if she had descended into a coma.

Silence prevailed as Rex stood beside her, confused and worried. The look in Sophia's eyes made it difficult for Rex to think clearly.

He picked up her phone, which had fallen to the floor, and dropped it back on the table.

He felt her pulse and tried to pull her forward, but Sophia slapped off his hand.

It was a painful slap, but Rex loved it. He loved the message that the slap portrayed. Sophia was physically fine.

"Talk to me. Let me help you. Remember everything we've talked about," he said pleadingly.

Sophia didn't respond to his utterance. She was cold, and her eyes looked incredibly pale.

"Please talk to me," he said, caressing her neck.

Sophia continued to keep her face forward, unflinching.

After stroking her neck, Rex dropped down on the floor and started massaging her feet, desperate to be of service to her.

She was still quiet but indulged him. Sophia was still looking toward the wall as if something was looking back at her.

Slowly, tears started to well up in her eyes. Rex didn't immediately notice because he was busy massaging her feet.

"Why? Why now?" Sophia asked, suddenly, impelling Rex to look up at her.

He saw the tears in her eyes, shook his head, and stood up from the floor. He sat on the handle of the chair and placed one hand on her shoulder.

"Why is life so unfair? Why does it take and take from some people and give so much more to others?" Sophia asked.

Rex was unresponsive but listened attentively. Tears started dribbling down from her eyes and down her face. Rex didn't try to dry her tears. Instead, he remained at her side, making himself available for her.

"She suffered and suffered until she couldn't afford to take it anymore. She didn't understand why life chose her to reveal its darkest side," Sophia's eyes glistened with more tears as she stared down at the floor, her shoulders slumping slightly as if the weight of her words pressed down on her. The pain etched on her face was undeniable, but there was a quiet determination in her expression, a resolve to keep speaking, even as the emotions threatened to overwhelm her. "She couldn't find an answer to that question until her death. She felt she was weak, but holding on to memories takes strength, doesn't it? It takes love. It takes faithfulness. It takes loyalty. My mom was loyal to her loved ones, but it didn't stop her from suffering. Now she's gone. Maybe now she'd find peace," Sophia sniffled.

Rex placed one hand on his brow, looming his face down slightly. He stood up and walked toward the glass wall, overtaken by grief.

"I wanted her to be at my wedding. I wanted her to have a feeling of the love between us. I wanted to create something beautiful inside her," Sophia said sadly.

Rex continued to back her, leaning his elbow against the wall as he slipped into solitude.

"Didn't she deserve to see me happy? Didn't she deserve to be at my wedding and share in my joy? Couldn't life have given her that one chance? What would it have cost life to let her live a little more? What would it have cost life to allow her share in a bit of sunshine before her death?" She sobbed.

Blobs of phlegm slipped out of her nose, joining in the congregation of tears slipping down her face. Sophia was crying like a child, utterly miserable as she considered the sudden death of her mom.

"She loved the engagement ring. She blessed it. How would I have known it was the last blessing she was giving me? I should have cherished it more. I should have cherished the kiss and spent more time with her. I should have taken her to a restaurant and allowed her to experience a romantic date one more time. I should have done more for her," Sophia said, crying. Her voice kept breaking, interrupted by frequent sniffles.

Rex turned toward her, his expression somber and resolute. Though his eyes were void of their usual warmth, they held a deep, quiet strength. His jaw was set, and his right hand was clenched in an effort to maintain control over the emotions swirling inside him. Even without tears, it was clear he felt the weight of the moment.

As he walked toward her, Sophia stood up from the chair, shaking and forcing him to increase the pace of his movement.

"I am so sorry," he said, weaving his hands across her back. "I know how much you loved her. I am so sorry," he said, holding on tightly to her.

She dropped her face on his chest and started making blubbering sounds.

Rex stroked her hair, wearing a sad, weary look. He didn't try to tell her to stop crying. It seemed he wanted her to cry. He wanted her to empty her grief in his presence. He wanted to stay with her, hold her hand, and assure her that the shackles of grief wouldn't be keeping her bound for so long.

"I should have done more for her. I waited too long. I was too focused on giving her a memorable wedding experience," Sophia said painfully.

"You loved her, Babe. You cherished her. I am sure she knew that. I am sure she knew how much you cared for her," Rex whispered in her ear and held her while she cried. Once she had calmed down, he picked her up and carried her to their bedroom. He gently laid her on the bed and slid in next to her, holding her tightly for the rest of the evening.

CHAPTER 10
The Wedding

The magnificent Cactus Hotel was a venue like no other, blending opulence with a touch of desert charm. The lobby, an expansive space that seated 200 guests, was bathed in natural light streaming through the skylight, casting a warm, golden hue over the room. The grand staircase, a masterpiece of marble and ironwork, spiraled gracefully upwards, each step inviting guests to ascend to new heights of elegance. The aisles, lushly carpeted in deep burgundy, were adorned with an abundance of sweet-smelling red roses, their petals perfectly arranged as if they had just fallen from a romantic dream. Above, an orchestra perched on an overhanging platform played *Giving It All to You* by Haley and Michaels, their harmonious melodies drifting down like a serenade, enveloping the entire lobby in a symphony of love and sophistication.

It was just the sound of music, but this sound was different.

It left the souls of the audience aloft with outstretched hands, comforted by the showers of memories and the smell of happiness.

Sophia was in the bride's room with her bridal party and dearest friend (and neighbor) from Cabo, Josh. He was the only one she would let do her hair. She did not want anyone else but him to do it because she knew it would be perfect and done with love. She was elated when he said he would fly out to be with her on this special day.

At the bottom of the grand staircase, the minister donned an all-white suit and stood before the guest, his bible opened to Amos 3:3. Rex stood just below the minister in his dapper, black tux and white, creaseless, long-sleeved shirt.

Rex's breathing was measured, and his excitement reached new depths. His eyes shone brightly amidst the slight wetness that prevailed within them. When more tears gathered in his left eye, a hand extended forward, wiping off the tears gathering at the corner of his eye. That hand belonged to Roger.

Roger wore the same tux as Rex. His black hair was sleek and combed back, and his expression showed a deep reverence for the occasion.

At the front row, David, Jazmin's husband, sat beside Allen, who was amongst Rex's groomsmen. The Groomsmen wore black suits exuding style and sophistication as they took their places.

At the edge of the row sat a young boy named Adam, just five years old and already taking his duties very seriously. Jack's son was a mini version of his father, dressed in a small tux that matched Jack's perfectly. Adam's small hands kept checking his briefcase, which proudly displayed the word "SECURITY" on it —his special job was to guard the wedding rings. His chest puffed out with pride as he wore a badge that read "Top Security." Even though being the ring bearer was a big responsibility for such a little guy, he took it in stride. Sitting beside Cynthia, his mother, who was one of the bridesmaids, gave him the comfort he needed. Adam's dark, sleek hair was neatly combed back, making him look like a miniature gentleman, just like his father. It was hard not to smile at the sight of him, so earnest and determined in his important role.

The sound of the orchestra made everyone in the room emotional. The song by Haley and Michaels couldn't have been played better in a way that mimicked a hymn and felt like the rendition of angels.

The presence of Sophia was presaged by the entrance of the flower girls, Bianca and Belinda– Jazmin's daughters, who sprayed rose petals from a little basket in front of them. The baskets were neatly weaved across their white, overflowing gowns to give them some stability. And their white pump shoes landed on the aisle majestically as they made their way down the grand staircase.

Behind the flower girls, Jack led Sophia down the grand staircase. Her father had passed years before, therefore not able to walk her down the aisle. She was so honored when her son Jack accepted the role of her father to walk her down the aisle. He wore a black tux and shaved his beard slightly to leave it clean and smooth. He took her hand and kept a smile on his face amidst the sound of the orchestra.

Sophia was emotional in her white, overflowing wedding

dress. Her body had become a roadmap of emotions. Sophia was as emotional as could be and kept her face forward, unwilling to check out the guest.

The sound of cheers erupted from a few lips, but Sophia had a feeling that she could burst into tears if she started looking around.

Her breathing was already heavy, and her face was flushed with excitement.

Edging a measured distance behind her, Jazmin, her maid of honor, straightened out Sophia's wedding dress, ensuring her movements were undeterred by anything on the staircase.

As Sophia drew closer and closer to the minister, Rex struggled to contain his emotions. Roger had to stand at his side at this point.

Sophia was now standing face to face with Rex.

Everyone waited for the orchestra to finish the song. And when they were done, a round of applause followed.

Julia was in tears. She kept wiping her eyes, as if in utter disbelief. Beside her, Caroline was emotional and elated by the spectacle before her.

The minister stepped forward and began to speak.

"Dearly beloved, we have gathered in the presence of the Lord to witness and bless the joining of Sophia and Rex in holy matrimony. In the book of Amos three, verse three, the Bible asks a question. Can two walk together unless they agree?" the minister asked gently.

Sophia started smiling, barely listening to the minister as she kept her eyes on Rex. The smile that emanated from her lips helped to translate the way Rex responded to the occasion. His tears of joy were slowly transfigured into vivid smiling.

His hands itched for her. He wanted to embrace her. Sophia and Rex were deafened by the message of the minister as they locked eyes.

They drew closer to each other as they exchanged their vows. Tears rolled down from Sophia's eyes just as Rex said, "I do." Her heart was full of joy.

When it was time to kiss, Sophia and Rex embraced first before they kissed. It was a short, soft kiss that venerated the venue, but they held hands after the kiss and looked toward the congregation, who cheered, stood on their feet, and clapped their hands.

It was the first time Sophia had an opportunity to look at the guests. She saw Julia and Caroline. She saw Elli jumping as she stretched her hands forward, with ten of her "Cabo Family" who flew in for the wedding. She could not believe her eyes. She looked around and saw all of Ronnie's family clapping and cheering. His two nephews were their ushers to seat people. So many friends of Rex's attended; it was so touching to see.

Seeing Elli brought tears to her eyes. Elli was supposed to miss the wedding. She had an important work meeting that made it difficult to travel to Texas today.

Sophia waved to Elli. "Thank you," she mouthed and started looking across the other faces in the room.

She was touched by the obvious aura of happiness that permeated the venue. Everyone was happy for her and Rex.

Suddenly, it occurred to her that there was no sign of Sabrina. She kept looking for a while before exhaling deeply, unwilling to let Sabrina's absence ruin the beauty and happiness that surrounded her. She was hoping she would surprise her and come.

The reception was just as spectacular. Round tables with adjoined, cushioned chairs were neatly spaced out. There was enough walking space in the large ballroom.

Rex and Sophia sat across a sprawling table on an overhung platform overlooking the guests at the round tables. They were joined by their wedding party.

The tables closest to the overhung platform were occupied by close friends and relatives. Sophia could see Elli, Julia, and Caroline sharing the table closest to the overhung platform. Allen and Rex's family shared the table next to them.

"The goddess of Cabo," Elli screamed from below, waving at Sophia, who smiled faintly at her.

In that moment, a popular band in San Angelo started to play from the other end of the overhung platform.

The sound of the guitar and the melodious voice of their lead singer took the guests unaware. Gradually, silence prevailed across the auditorium as most of the guests were mesmerized by the inimitable voice of the lead singer.

Roger was especially fascinated by this performance. He held his glass of champagne up and sang along, nodding his head and gesticulating with his other hand.

Jazmin walked over to Sophia and handed her the phone. To Sophia's surprise, it was Sabrina on FaceTime.

"Hi, Mom!" Sabrina greeted excitedly.

"Hi, honey," Sophia responded warmly.

"I'm so sorry I couldn't make it to your wedding! I really tried. I was planning to fly out and surprise you, but I couldn't get a flight at the last minute," Sabrina explained, looking disappointed.

"I understand, sweetheart, but you're missed so much," Sophia reassured her.

"Jazmin showed me around the wedding before giving you the phone. It's absolutely beautiful, Mom, and everyone seems to be having an amazing time," Sabrina said with a big smile.

"It truly was the most beautiful wedding, everything was perfect!" Sophia agreed.

"You look happy, Mom," Sabrina observed.

"I really am, honey," Sophia said, beaming.

"Well, I'll let you get back to your guests. I love you, Mom," Sabrina said.

"I love you too, and thank you for the call. It meant the world to me. Bye for now," Sophia replied.

Rex dropped one hand on Sophia's shoulder and leaned toward her. He kissed her cheek and suddenly started singing along with the band.

At the end of the song, some of the guests drifted toward the buffet on the left side of the ballroom.

There were servers at designated positions in the ballroom. The servers wore uniforms that made it easy to detect them.

As Sophia looked toward the guests amidst the sound of music, she was pleased by the orderliness and organization. Everything was in order. Her caterer was City Café and Bakery, which was the best in San Angelo. She did an impeccable job with the food, the decorations, the cake, and especially the ambiance.

Two other songs played before Jazmin took the mic and stepped forward. She had a big smile on her face and regarded both Rex and Sophia proudly.

"Good evening, everyone and thank you so much for joining us for this very special occasion. My name is Jazmin, and I've known the bride for many years," Jazmin started, taking a step forward with a look of amusement adorning her flushed face.

"Being the oldest daughter of the bride, I have seen her through various moments- the highs and the lows.. For those of you who don't know my mom very well, just think of her as a mix of Paula Dean and the Energizer Bunny.", she joked. "She loves to play ready, set, cook with items found in the house, and it somehow comes out as a gourmet meal. It's like magic. She is also always on the go and busy. She loves to travel and try new things. She is super creative and loves to take care of people, especially when it comes to feeding them," Jazmin gestured, taking a side look at Sophia, who was adorning a blushed smile.

"Rex, I can tell you two things: you will never be again. You will never be hungry and bored," she said, taking a pause as some of the guests chuckled. She grinned delightfully.

"Also, my mom isn't fancy like AppleBees on date night. She's fancy, like a Michelin-star restaurant on a cruise ship in the Mediterranean." Jazmin held the short pause and she peered across the room to find Sophia holding her fingers to the corners of her eyes. Jazmin smiled at her.

"My mom can really rough it up in the country. She can hunt, fish, and camp with the best of them. I would, however, put money on the fact that she has either worn or seriously considered wearing camo stilettos while hunting." The room exploded with laughter from the guests as Rex chuckled and intertwined his hand with Sophia's.

"But whether it's venison, rabbit, quail, or fish, she will

make it taste like heaven," Jazmin said proudly, and a round of applause sifted from the guests.

"Soon after meeting Rex, my mom told me about him. She was really excited, and I could tell right away that this was going to be serious because she would light up when talking about him. My mom would go on and on about the funny things he would say and how much fun he was. Then she would try to explain some of the jokes, and I'll just tell you that they go right over my head, but as long as they get it, that's what matters," Jazmin exclaimed as more laughter erupted from all corners of the room.

"If you follow my mom on social media, you'll know that it has been a Hallmark movie whirlwind romance of picnics at the ranch, and rescuing baby lambs. But they have been there for each other when difficult news was delivered or through losing a loved one," Jazmin said, taking a deep breath as her voice became tinged with emotions. Her eyes welled up with tears, and she dropped her face slightly.

The guests clapped loudly. Julia and Jack stood up, applauding Jazmin as she succumbed to emotions. Caroline screamed her name.

Jazmin raised her face up, smiling at the guests. She nodded and wiped off the tears in her eyes with her other hand.

"My grandparents were married and in love for their entire adult lives," Jazmin continued, her voice becoming firm and steady.

"They were married at eighteen. So, if anyone knows about being successful in marriage, it's them. First of all, my grandmother had the patience of an actual saint, and my grandfather understood how much truth is in the statement 'happy wife, happy life,'" Jazmin said, turning to Sophia and Rex who were now visibly brought to tears.

"And because my wonderful grandparents are only here in spirit with us this evening. Rex, I will do the honor of passing along what my grandpa told David and I on our wedding day: the secret to a successful marriage is that each person has to always give ninety percent but only expect ten percent in return. Do that, he said, and you will both have a wonderful, successful marriage...and don't forget happy wife, happy life." Jazmin grinned.

She took a step forward. "Rex, welcome to the family. Mom, we love you and are so happy for you both. Everyone, please join me and lift up your glass to the bride and groom! Cheers!"

Jack walked up to her, giving her a tight embrace.

Sophia stood up, applauding excitedly. After applauding for a while, she drifted toward Jazmin and Jack and embraced them together. "Thank you, baby. I love you," Sophia said, kissing Jazmin's cheek.

After a few songs played, Rex took the mic. He turned to the guests and nodded his head like a fighter in a WrestleMania ring.

"I am so lucky," he started, nodding. "I am so lucky," he repeated, eliciting a round of applause from the guests.

"You see; I have always understood love. I know what it looks like when it is true and sincere. But I also know what it can look like when people let their bias and selfishness get in the way.

When I met Sophia, I prayed about it. I fell on my knees because our first conversation was so beautiful. I am here today to tell you that God answered that prayer," Rex said, nodding.

"God listened and led me to her. Sophia is from God. My wife is from God," Rex exclaimed, turning toward Sophia. He drifted toward her and kissed her cheek.

All the guests stood up and clapped their hands as Rex kissed Sophia.

She returned to the stage and exuded a big smile as he scratched his mustache ever so slightly.

"Jazmin is right about her. She is a great cook. I can feel the extra pounds her meals have left on my stomach. And when I feel like things are getting difficult, I think about her. I think about her sacrifices. I think about her strength. My wife is not a quitter, and it would be stupid if her man cannot imbibe such a virtue," Rex added, turning to Sophia.

"I love you so much, Sophia. From the first day, I have loved you. I have imagined being married to you several times. You brought back butterflies in my stomach. You became God's apology for all the heartbreaks and pain I have endured."

Rex dropped the mic and moved toward Sophia, embracing her and kissing her cheek before leaving another kiss on her lips.

When Sophia took the mic and came on stage, there was loud screaming in the ballroom. Caroline, Julia, Elli, and other acquaintances from Texas and Cabo cheered her.

She smiled, her green eyes shining with a wet glint. She was impressed with the sound of applause and waited for it to die down.

"To be honest, I don't know where to start from. I wanted to write a speech for this occasion but decided at the last moment that I was going to speak from my heart," Sophia said in a sonorous voice.

"If you understand pain and grief, you'd know that some pain never goes away. You have to keep them at your side when you experience moments of joy. Pain taught me to cherish joyful moments because nothing is truly guaranteed," Sophia said seriously.

"When I lost my husband, I couldn't get back into the dating pool because I was always disenchanted at the talking stages. But when I met Rex, I had a feeling- a hunch you could say, that I was starting something that wouldn't follow the awful talking stages I had grown accustomed to. He was funny. His dating experiences were funny and awful, but they made him more receptive to me. According to him, those experiences prepared him for me," Sophia said, retaining her serious, calm voice.

"Rex brought all my imaginations to life. He gave me assurances that he wasn't even sure about actualizing, but he believed that he could go even deeper in loving me. I haven't seen anything like it. He taught me how to love intensely. And when I felt stuck, he made suggestions about sacrifices that he could make to make me feel better," she said, taking a step to the side. She looked towards Rex, who had a huge smile plastered to his face. His eyes shone with the same wetness as her own.

"He is proactive. When I lost my mom, he was there for me. He would embrace me, sing to me, and console me with words that made me feel less guilty."

Her voice broke as she said the next words. "Rex understands love in a way that is eerie and crazy," Sophia turned to face Rex again. .

"I know things haven't always been easy. I know there are rough rides waiting for us in the future, but I'm always going to love you, Rex. I am always going to appreciate the way you love me. Thank you so much for coming into my life," Sophia exclaimed now completely in the verge of tears.

Yet still, Sophia managed to remain calm and steady. She looked across the faces of the applauding guests, bowing ever so slightly.

The sound of music grew louder as the people in the ballroom danced. Sophia drifted from her table onto the overhung platform and joined her sisters and Elli on the dance floor.

The dancing grew intense, interspersed by whining waists and screaming voices.

Sophia and Rex danced together, taking up slightly unrestrained moves as Sophia's sisters cheered.

Julia drew close to Sophia, holding her close in an awkward embrace.

"This is such a beautiful wedding, Sophia. Mom would be so proud," Julia said, pulling away from Sophia.

Sophia was touched by her words and felt it unusual amidst the dancing. She remained still for a while, smiling as she thought about Rose and the moment she had kissed her ring.

The celebration continued late into the night as people danced until after midnight. Gradually, guests began to leave, and Sophia and Rex made their way to their hotel room. After a relaxing shower, they slipped into bed together.

Rex turned to her, a tender smile on his face. "I love you, Mrs. Presley," he said softly.

"I love you too, Mr. Presley," Sophia responded, her voice filled with affection.

Rex gazed into Sophia's eyes, his touch gentle and sensual, sending shivers down her spine. She let out a soft moan, whispering, "We get to do this for the rest of our lives."

"Yes, we do," Rex agreed, his voice filled with love.

He kissed her passionately, rolling on top of her. They made love for hours, their connection deepening as they embraced each other for the first time as husband and wife.

CHAPTER 11

Juggling Homes

It was the fourth time Sophia had gone back to Cabo in the space of a couple of months. She was in her car, dressed corporately in a camisole top and an all-black suit.

Her face was weary, and her eyes had a few bleary splotches. She dropped her face on the steering wheel, biting hard on her bottom lip.

She made her way towards the familiar door of her apartment. With a deep breath, she slid the key into the lock and turned it. The door gave a soft creak as she nudged it open, the scent of the apartment—slightly musty but unmistakably hers—wafting out to meet her. She paused in the doorway, taking in the comforting but distant sense of home before stepping inside. She went straight into her bedroom. Sophia dropped face down on the bed and dozed off.

It was a deep sleep that featured snoring and drooling. She was woken up prematurely by the sound of her phone ringing. She pushed the phone aside and tried to sleep again.

However, it was difficult to gain the momentum she had lost. Sophia exuded a long sigh after trying in vain to sleep again.

There was an obvious glare in her eyes as she picked up the phone and looked at the phone screen. There were four missed calls from Rex.

Sophia stared at the phone number for a long time before sending a message.

Rex. I'm trying to rest. It's been a difficult day.

After sending the message, she went into the bathroom and stood under the shower, listening to the sound of water hitting the floor.

Sophia barely mingled with any thought in the bathroom. When she returned to the bedroom, she quickly put on a night-dress and tried to sleep again.

Sophia closed her eyes and tried to remain calm, but her mind became active.

Suddenly, she rolled toward the side of the bed and picked up her phone from the top of the cabinet beside the bed. Sophia checked the message she had just sent to Rex and felt bad about it. She felt it was dismissive and created the impression that Rex was disturbing her peace.

She thought about sending another message but decided, while she was already typing, to wait for Rex's response.

She lay back in her bed and tried to sleep again, but she didn't manage any success in that either.

Sophia stood up from the bed and walked into the bathroom and back to the bedroom without a clear purpose.

She paced around the bedroom for a while before traipsing down to the living room.

Sophia was tired and felt a little broken.

She fell down in her lounge chair and tried to sleep again. This time, she succeeded. Sophia slept for a while, but when she woke up, she was still tired.

She hurried back to the bedroom and found that Rex hadn't replied to her message. Sophia sighed and sent another message.

I didn't manage to catch any real rest. Are you ok?

After sending the message, she kept the phone on her thigh and waited for his response.

After waiting for twenty minutes, Sophia dialed his number. Surprisingly, it was switched off.

She threw the phone on the bed and changed into a white dress. She went back into her car and drove away from her home.

Sophia had no real location in mind. She simply wanted to drive and see whether it would make her feel better. Since coming to Cabo for the fourth time in a couple months, her communication with Rex had grown leaner and leaner because of her hectic work routine and his surprising nonchalance.

Sophia took a moment to immerse herself in the beauty weaved across the road. She drove slowly, checking out the bars, restaurants, and random gatherings. These were the lively features that set Cabo apart from San Angelo.

She saw a couple dancing outside a bar, stopped at the roadside, and watched them. In that moment, the sun started to set, leaving touches of its orange glow on the bar.

It started to feel like the dancing couple were figments of her imagination. It was even more beautiful because the couple was uninterested in the rays of sunset. They were so caught up in their little dance and detached themselves from the moving poetry they inadvertently created.

Sophia kept her eyes on the couple until they noticed her attention and became unnerved by it. They stopped dancing and spoke in low tones.

Sophia detected the suspicion in their eyes and drove away to make them feel better. After driving for five minutes, Sophia stopped at the roadside and dialed Rex's number.

This time, the call went through.

"Hey, Babe. How are you doing?" she asked.

"What?" Rex asked.

Sophia shook her head disappointedly as the sound of music wafted out from Rex's end.

"Go somewhere quiet," Sophia responded.

"I can't hear you, Babe. I am out with Roger. I will call you when I get home," Rex said, abruptly ending the call.

Sophia took a deep breath, dropped her phone on the passenger seat beside her, and started slapping the steering wheel. "He'd rather do that than speak to his wife?", she exclaimed.

Sophia's respiration was raspy, and she struggled to calm down and think clearly.

"This is what I get? For all of the sacrifices- this is what I get?" she said and took a deep breath.

Her eyes caught a sign at the roadside that reminded her that she wasn't so far away from Elli's home.

She turned on the ignition and drove to Elli's. When Sophia reached Elli's home, she took out her phone and texted her.

I am outside your house. Are you there?

Sophia sat back in the car, waiting for Elli's response. It came a few minutes later.

Yeah. I am getting ready to go out.

Sophia stared into the distance as she tried to count her breaths.

In through my nose, out through my mouth.

Elli came outside and walked toward Sophia's car. She wore a black dress, opened the door, and joined her inside the car. Sophia sucked in a deep breath.

"Are you alright?" Elli asked immediately sensing that Sophia didn't look her usual, calm self.

"Yes," Sophia shifted uncomfortably in her seat and turned to face Elli.

"Are you sure?" Elli could tell something was seriously wrong.

"Where are you going?" Sophia asked abruptly in an attempt to divert the attention away from how she was feeling.

"Just a bar. To meet some of our friends." Elli trailed, raising an eyebrow at her friend seated beside her.

"God! I haven't had time to thank them individually," Sophia responded rather too cheerfully.

"Do you have to? You thanked us at your wedding. You had

time for us. I think everyone appreciated the way you behaved." Elli chuckled.

"I will just go with you," Sophia said as she stared at Elli hoping she could help her get her mind off of Rex and the party. And Roger. And the nonchalance–

"Are you sure you're alright?" Elli questioned again breaking her trance.

"Oh, of course. I am very fine," Sophia smiled.

Elli was obviously not convinced, and Sophia wasn't doing a great job at concealing any of it. Elli could see right through it.

"I know something's up, Sophia." Elli glanced over at her as she said this and paused.

"But I want you to take your time. I will listen when you want to talk," she continued.

Sophia smiled weakly at her and pressed on the accelerator.

Sophia pulled up outside the fancy bar that everyone was getting together in and followed Elli inside.

The bar was sprawling and had an active MC coordinating the music and spicing up the general activity in the bar. Sometimes, the MC drew the attention of some of the guests, complimenting them.

Elli led Sophia to the far wall, taking their friends by surprise. They were excited to see Sophia, who struggled to match their excitement. There was hugging, kissing, and exchanging of pleasantries. The ladies spent the next twenty minutes talking about Sophia's wedding.

There were nine ladies at the table, and every single one of them was dressed fashionably.

Elli handed Sophia a tequila shot.

"Take this. It will make you feel better," Elli said.

Sophia took the shot glass from her hand, stared at it for a while, and took a drink.

After taking the shot, Sophia took out her phone and took a sneak at the time. It was seven-twenty-five PM, but there was still no response from Rex.

When Sophia turned back to the table, Elli was looking at her.

Sophia feigned a smile and moved her body slightly.

Two ladies at the table stood up and danced vigorously. The MC noticed and praised them, encouraging them to continue dancing.

"What has Rex done?" Elli asked.

"He hasn't done anything," Sophia responded and picked up another tequila shot. She took a quick drink.

Elli turned away from Sophia and started dancing. From the way she danced, it was easy to see that dancing had always been on Elli's agenda. Also, Sophia was happy that she hadn't allowed her feelings to come in the way of Ellis's initial intentions.

Watching Elli dance made Sophia smile. She was slightly cheerful, but it was difficult to join them in dancing because she was actually tired and couldn't stop wondering why Rex was taking too long to reach her.

As Sophia became closeted in her mind, everyone at the tables around her danced. The ladies were rocking one another, and Sophia was the only one sitting at their table.

She felt a bump on her left shoulder from a dancing lady and thought about dancing. Perhaps dancing would make her feel better, but Sophia decided against this move, deciding to continue sitting.

"Come on, beautiful ladies. Dance. Thinking about your problems won't solve them," the MC said.

Sophia had a feeling that he was referring to her, but she was not in the mood to respond to small talk. She didn't even turn toward the MC, who uttered other encouraging words.

When the ladies were done dancing, four of them joined Sophia in her car. She drove them to their respective homes before driving down to Elli's home.

"Thank you so much," Elli said, placing one hand on her shoulder. "Are you sure everything is fine?"

Sophia felt like she couldn't handle the feeling anymore. She burst out, "I feel like I am feeling pressured."

"Pressured? By what?" Elli was taken aback by her statement. She didn't know what she was expecting, but it wasn't this.

"By everything." Sophia said softly.

"Is it Rex? Has he done anything?" Elli's tone turned defensive.

"I feel I am starting to hate the fact that I keep traveling back and forth. It is really stressful." Sophia sniffled as she said this. "I don't know how much longer I can do this?"

"But you chose this life. You knew it wouldn't be easy." Elli said as she glanced at Sophia.

"Yes, but sometimes I really wish San Angelo felt more like Cabo. I've struggled to build my own friendships here. Back in Cabo, I was always surrounded by my friends, always doing something together. We were more like family. Now, I have our neighbors and his friends, but I don't have anyone who I can really talk to. Don't get me wrong—they're all amazing. They treat me so well, and they're always so kind and supportive.

They come to our parties, and we always have a good time, but they are all so busy in their own lives," Sofia admitted, nervously fidgeting with her fingers.

"What are you going to do about it?" Elli asked as Sophia leaned back against the seat.

"I don't know. It has been more than eight months since our wedding, and I just feel like I'm losing it." Sophia stared out the window as the horizon became enveloped in various shades of ink.

"Sophia, you know I love you. We talked about this. You can't succumb now. Remember your wedding speech? You kept talking about sacrifices, because that's what's important in any marriage." Elli stated gently caressing Sophia's shoulder.

"I know, but I'm tired. I am really tired, Elli. A part of me feels like I can't take it anymore. I am starting to feel unappreciated." Sophia sighed.

"Why are you sounding like this? Are you thinking about getting a divorce?" Elli asked plainly.

"No. I haven't thought about that at all." Sophia hadn't thought about a divorce. She just knew something was wrong. She didn't want to let go of Rex, but things weren't how they were supposed to be.

"But that's exactly where you're headed," Elli responded.

"I love Rex. I really do. And I don't want him to relocate to Cabo. His production is getting higher, and it would be devilish to want him to relocate at this point." Sophia crossed her arms.

"I don't know how to advise you on this one, Sophia. Maybe you need to tell him how you feel." Elli always did know what to say, and the only advice she had was probably the right thing to do.

"He knows how I feel about living in San Angelo, but he doesn't look like he can do anything about it. I feel like I'm the only one making real sacrifices." Sophia felt more and more defeated as the conversation continued and she sunk into her seat.

"That is the wrong way to see things. Remember he wanted to come live with you in Cabo?" Elli asked.

"Yes. But that was long ago now. I can't think of making that suggestion anymore. I would feel too guilty if I did. Also, I don't think he'd like it." Sophia glanced over at Elli who was staring at her with a frown perched on her lips.

"Maybe you need to change the way you feel about San Angelo. Maybe you need to open your heart to it and make it your home. You did that with Cabo." Elli was trying to make her feel better about the situation.

Sophia sighed. "I had you, Elli. I had our other friends–"

"Now you have Rex," Elli cut in, interrupting Sophia. "You chose him. He loves you. Your presence has is the reason for his increase in focus and production. Maybe you just need to give it a little more time and find a way to find a common ground where you can work on the decisions you've made for your marriage."

Sophia was thinking about her conversation with Elli when she got home. The time was edging past nine in the evening, but there was still no response from Rex.

Sophia tried his number a few times, but there was no response from his end.

She was frustrated, distraught, and angry. Rex hadn't ever stayed out this long without reaching out to her. And Sophia mingled with several thoughts. She wondered whether Rex was out with another woman but quickly shaved off this thought.

She decided to call Roger. Roger answered, but the sound of music made it difficult to hear him.

"What is happening?" Sophia wondered. Sophia was holding this thought when she dozed off in the lounge chair.

Sophia woke up around one AM and immediately reached for her phone on the stool beside her. There was no message from Rex. She was infuriated, but there was no distortion to her expression as she looked at her phone.

Really? I thought you would get back to me when you return? What are you up to? Why is there music there? What is this?

Sophia left the lounge chair and went to her bedroom. She lay face up in her bed, but sleep didn't come.

She was thinking, accommodating thoughts that had no business being on her mind. She wondered whether she was becoming miserable, whether she had inadvertently made life difficult for herself by anchoring the decision about her marriage on love.

CHAPTER 12

Misunderstandings

The next day, Sophia got to San Angelo in the afternoon. There was still no message from Rex. Sophia was in her car headed to his ranch when she eventually received his message.

Sophia swiped off his message, deciding not to read it. Tears gathered in her eyes, but she remained calm. After a while, she went back to the message and read it.

> I am so sorry for not reaching you last night. I got drunk. It was a stupid mistake. Roger invited some of the boys over and we had a drink after watching a football game. Since it is Saturday today, we thought we should do a little more carousing. It got out of hand. I didn't know when I went to sleep. It's crazy. I woke up past twelve. I hope you're still returning today. Please let me know.

Sophia was not amused after reading his text. Rex hadn't ever drunk himself into a stupor when she was around him. Hence, she wondered whether there was more to his story. Sophia recognized Rex's intelligence and sense of invention. Hence, it was easy to think that he was imbued with the right qualities to come up with excuses that were difficult to disprove.

I am coming,

Sophia texted back.

When Sophia reached the ranch, she walked straight inside the house. Rex was not inside, but Sophia didn't exactly bother.

There was wine, pasta, and sauce at the dining table, but Sophia went straight to the bathroom, took a shower, and went to bed.

When she woke up, Rex was sitting in the bed and looking straight at her face. Sophia was startled by his presence because her thoughts were slightly uncoordinated when she woke up. Sophia woke up thinking that she was still in Cabo.

She took a long look at Rex and rubbed the back of her right hand across her eyes.

"I will just microwave what I prepared for you," Rex said, kissing her forehead before leaving her side.

Sophia sat up in the bed without a trace of joy on her face. Although she was angry with Rex, she couldn't bring herself to lash out at him. Shouting, screaming, and quarreling hadn't previously featured in their relationships. Hence, it felt out of place to rely on methods that they had deemed unnecessary in resolving issues.

The smell of sauce wafted toward her as she left the bed. The house had taken on an entirely new look since the wedding.

Sophia had completely remodeled the house. It had taken up to six months to implement her plans. She added an outdoor kitchen and even a swimming pool.

"Come on, Babe. Come eat," Rex said invitingly.

Sophia looked across the walls, cabinets, and focused on the decoration she had done in the house. Focusing on the decorations made it easy to not consider her reservations about Rex's behavior the previous evening.

Sophia sat at the dining table and started eating. Rex was sitting beside her.

He was opening the bottle of wine when Sophia raised one hand up.

"I don't want to drink," she said in a hoarse, deep voice.

The sound of her voice immediately made Rex flinch, as if he was worried.

Sophia continued to eat. She was hungry and the food was actually delicious.

"You know a cattle client visited recently. He was really impressed with what you've done to the house. He couldn't believe our house had taken such a beautiful look," Rex said excitedly.

Sophia smiled without responding.

"He wants to know if you will be able to make a duplex look just as beautiful. I think he is really serious," Rex added.

Sophia filled a glass with water and took a gulp. She turned to Rex, glimpsed at his brown eyes, and sat back in her chair.

"We can talk about that later," Sophia said, her voice remaining hoarse and terrible.

"Are you alright?" Rex asked.

"I just want to rest," Sophia responded and moved to the bed.

She lay down and weaved her hands around her stomach. Sophia closed her eyes but wasn't actually feeling sleepy.

Rex came to bed and sat beside her.

"Is this about last evening? I am sorry for not calling you, Babe," Rex said seriously.

Sophia turned to him, her expression as serious as could be.

"I just want to rest," she responded and closed her eyes again.

REX WOULD LOOK AT HER CONSTANTLY TRYING TO figure out how she was feeling, Sophia gathered. Her behaviour did not showcase the vitality that followed their interactions.

Sophia said only what was needed and spent more time reading her books and sleeping. The times they spent together grew leaner and leaner.

It was so bad that Sophia started spending time alone in the field, stargazing. The desire to carry Rex along started to fade away.

Notwithstanding, they ate together and slept in the same bed.

On this particular day, Sophia took a stroll to the barn and watched as Rex kept giving instructions to facilitate an effective way to brand a steer.

Rex met her, smiled, and waved at her. Sophia waved back, but there was no hint of a smile on her face.

She returned to the house and walked around the house, her hands clasped behind her.

Sophia considered the decoration plan of the client Rex had talked about, and wondered whether getting busy in San Angelo could ease her into fully imbibing the subtleties of the town.

She realized that she felt way better when she was still decorating their house. For six months, she was free from the tormenting shackles of loneliness.

Her trance was broken when Rex entered the house, suddenly grinning widely at her..

"I will be going out tonight. A friend just paid off his mortgage and wants to organize a little get-together," Rex said, moving toward the bedroom.

"Is that so?" Sophia responded.

"What do you mean?" Rex asked.

"What do I mean? Seriously? I am so fucking lonely here, and any chance you get, you run off with your friends?" Sophia responded, raising her voice.

"Run off with my friends? What do you mean?" Rex stared at his wife blankly.

"You know what? Just fucking go, okay. And when you get there, you can just fucking stay there till morning. Get drunk and forget you have a wife." Sophia shouted. She knew this had been built up for too long. She had finally let loose.

"How can you say that to me?" Rex asked, raising his voice.

"Don't ask me that stupid question. You know what you need to do, but you just don't care. You don't care about how I feel. I have been to Cabo four times in the last couple of months, but what do you care? I come back every time because I want to spend time with you. But I come here and see my husband doing what he likes, thinking about himself alone." Sophia cried, with her voice breaking between sentences. She was not used to this. She didn't like it.

"What the fuck is wrong with you?" Rex barked at her.

"What is wrong with me? Ask yourself that question, Rex. I am sure you will find better answers. Don't you see what you're doing to me? Don't you fucking have eyes? Are you blind?" Sophia retorted.

"I knew you were up to something. You know what? I am out of here. You keep pissing me off." Rex said as he slammed the door shut.

"Yes. Go away. Do what you are good at. Go the fuck away." Sophia shouted after him.

Rex shook his head as he walked towards the car in deep thought. He quickly unlocked the door and slid into the driver's seat. Without missing a beat, he inserted the key into the ignition and turned it, the engine roaring to life with a low, familiar rumble. He shifted into gear and pulled out of the parking space, the tires crunching over the gravel as he drove away, the road stretching out before him.

As soon as she saw him leave, Sophia dropped on a couch and placed her hands on her face as tears welled up in her eyes.

After crying for a while, Sophia thought about

the nature of the fight with Rex. It was the first time they had shown a bit of unrestrained hostility toward each other.

Sophia thought about messaging Jazmin but decided against it. She took her time to think about the situation, the words exchanged, and the more she thought about it, Sophia struggled to find a way around the problem. It started to feel like they could only go downhill from here.

Sophia picked up her phone and texted Elli.

> I shouted at him and we just had a serious argument. I have never gotten into a fight with him. I don't know what to do.

Sophia took a deep breath and ran one hand across her face, wiping her tears.

Moments later, Sophia went to the dining table and started drinking from the bottle of wine that Rex had left there.

Sophia drank straight from the bottle, taking large slugs as her eyes reddened with grief and gloom.

Elli responded to her text when Sophia was already halfway through the bottle.

> This is crazy. I think you need to calm down now. I am sure he will try to talk about the matter. Listening is important at this point. It can be the difference between failing and succeeding. Here for you. xx

Sophia dropped the phone and continued drinking from the bottle of wine. She thought about their big wedding and her speech. She thought about Julia whispering in her ear about how her mom would be so proud of her.

Sophia gritted her teeth and picked up her phone, rereading Ellis's message. She dropped the phone back on the dining table and staggered forward. Her knees were weak from heavy consumption of wine, and her hands shook ever so slightly.

Sophia staggered back to the straight-back chair at the dining table and sat down.

"How long will he stay away?" she muttered to herself.

This question pushed her toward wondering whether she was staring at the beginning of the end. Her palpitation gathered pace, and Sophia was desperately sad.

She reckoned she would have to live in shame for a long time if she and Rex divorced after their first real fight. It just didn't make sense.

Again, she stood up from the chair, reeling from the weakness in her knees, but Sophia was tired and sleepy. The alcohol made things worse. It magnified her fear.

Sophia staggered unusually a few times as she made her way to the bed. Her upper body was steeped forward, and it looked like she could tip herself over and fall face down on the floor, but Sophia managed to reach the bed.

Sophia fell face down in the bed. Her legs were still on the floor. She was too tired to raise them. She closed her eyes and had a flash of herself dancing in her wedding dress before sleep took over, ensuring an easy slip into unconsciousness.

CHAPTER 13
Finding Balance

Sophia felt tongues licking her face from both sides. It was an eerie feeling that didn't follow the dimension of most of her dreams. For a moment, she was stuck in the position between waking and sleeping, and it started to feel like she couldn't wean herself from this position.

Sophia continued to feel sad amidst the strange feeling. Suddenly, she opened her eyes and saw two white toy Maltese puppies at her side. They were fluffy and looked innocuous.

Sophia was startled and tried to creep away from them. For a moment, she wondered whether she had suddenly descended into an unusual dream that mimicked reality.

Her breathing was fast and heavy, and the dogs regarded her innocently and wagged their tails. They drew closer to her again.

"I got them," a voice said from behind the bed.

Once again, Sophia was startled. She tilted her face up and looked over her shoulder.

Rex was leaning against the head of the bed and wearing a solemn, thoughtful look.

He came to the bed, picked up the male dog, and stroked his back.

"When I was a boy, I used to have a dog. I called him Boots because he loved to sleep in my dad's old boots when he was small. I grew up with Boots, loved him, and took care of him. I spent so much time with him. Roger was around at the time, but Boots felt like my best friend, you know. We even slept in the same bed." He took a brief pause before he continued.

"But he died one day. Boots died in his sleep. It was a horrifying moment for me. I couldn't make sense of the death of such a lovely, beautiful dog. I felt other people deserved to die in his place, but Boots died of old age. And since then, I have stopped being keen on dogs. What was the use of having pets if they were going to die of old age at some point? Old age that isn't really old enough for me," Rex said softly.

He turned to Sophia, who was still trying to connect the story of Rex's dead dog to the presence of these two new dogs.

"You know, when I drove away, I stopped in a Walmart parking lot and saw this woman with a sign selling purebreed Maltese. It wasn't deliberate. I just needed a place to think, but then I realized that you are right. I haven't been exactly great to you in San Angelo. I haven't integrated you into my small community of friends. How can you make friends if I don't do more?" Rex asked, looking down slightly.

"I know you miss Cabo. I actually think you should go there when you can, sort out your business, mingle with your friends. But I realize that I am not usually myself when you're not around. If I was a beast, I think your absence would set me loose. I would never go out and overdrink if I knew you were waiting for me at home. So, I figured that I have been struggling to maintain the kind of communication we've always maintained when you are away," Rex said, taking a deep breath.

"I know this is not the first time it has happened, but I believe I should put myself in a position where you don't have to worry so much about me when you are away. Not putting myself in a good position is selfish because it kills your ability to really enjoy yourself in Cabo. I have a feeling it is why you keep coming back on the weekend even though you should stay a month and finish up with that contract," Rex said, looking up at her.

There were changes in Sophia's expression. His explanation made so much sense and explained some of the things she hadn't been able to detect in her own introspection.

"So, when I saw that lady with the puppies, it occurred to me that we could add a bit of spark in our relationship if I got another dog. My experience with Boots was fascinating, and I think having these two dogs would make me want to stay inside when you are not around. It would keep our communication intact. It would make it easy for you to be in Cabo without feeling the need to run back to me before finishing your obligations," Rex said.

Sophia picked up the female puppy and stroked her back. She felt so much better and started to feel a bit guilty as she noticed the remorse on Rex's face. "I am also sorry. I shouldn't have spoken to you in that manner," Sophia said apologetically.

"I understand. Sometimes, these kinds of fights are necessary to put things in the right place. I am not sure I would have placed myself under immense surveillance if I didn't have this fight with you," Rex responded.

"You should have told me about Boots. He was clearly a big part of your childhood," Sophia said thoughtfully and continued to stroke the back of the white, fluffy puppy.

"Yeah. I should have done that. But there are times when we struggle to talk about some memories," Rex responded.

"Have you named them?" Sophia asked. She felt a headachy sensation at the back of her head, but Sophia was inured to it as she looked straight at him.

"No. I wanted us to name them together," Rex responded, smiling.

"Okay. Name the male one. I will name this one," Sophia said, stroking the back of the female puppy.

"Does Spike sound good?" Rex asked.

"It sounds like a name for a rugged dog," Sophia laughed.

"He looks rugged," Rex said, lifting him up slightly. He stroked the corner of his ear and turned to Sophia.

"What are you naming that one?" he asked.

"Fifi," Sophia said quickly.

"That sounds really sweet. Did you always have that name in mind?" Rex asked.

"It was the first thought that came to me when I woke up and saw her," Sophia responded.

"To be honest, she looks like a Fifi," Rex responded, chuckling.

Sophia leaned toward Rex and embraced him. "Thank you so much. Thank you for coming through when I needed you to," Sophia said as tears welled up in her eyes.

Rex nodded and stroked her back. "I can't believe I feel so much better now. I mean, this is actually how I have been feeling for some time. I just didn't see it that way." Rex smiled, nodding.

Sophia turned to Rex curiously. "Are you still going to the party?" she asked.

"I don't know. To be honest, I don't feel like it, but I think we should go. I would only go if you'd come with me," Rex responded.

Sophia smiled, pleased by his response. She could see that Rex was already implementing the changes he had decided to bring to their marriage.

"Of course I will go with you, but what about the dogs?" Sophia asked.

"We can take them along. Besides, we won't be staying for long," Rex responded.

Sophia nodded, standing up from the couch.

"I better get dressed then," she said and moved toward him. Sophia kissed his cheek. "Thank you so much for today," she said and kissed his lips.

A few days after Rex and Sophia made up, the tension between them had finally eased, and Sophia found herself feeling lighter than she had in months. She had taken Rex's words to heart, realizing that she needed to make her time in San Angelo more meaningful, not just for him, but for herself as well. Sitting at the kitchen table with a cup of coffee, she flipped open her notebook, staring down at the sketches she had drawn of their two new puppies, Spike and Fifi.

"I've been thinking," she said, glancing up as Rex entered the room. "About how I can make better use of my time when I'm here."

Rex smiled as he leaned against the counter, his eyes warm and supportive. "Yeah? What did you come up with?"

Sophia's face lit up as she pushed the notebook towards him. "Children's books. I've been sketching out some ideas for stories with Spike and Fifi as the main characters. I think it could be really fun, and it'll give me something to focus on when I'm not in Cabo."

Rex picked up the notebook, flipping through the pages with a thoughtful expression. "I love this idea, Sophia. The kids are going to adore these stories. What's the first one about?"

"The first one is about bullying," Sophia explained, her voice growing more animated as she spoke. "I want to teach kids about kindness and standing up for others. I've already outlined a story where Spike learns to stand up to a bigger dog who's been picking on FiFi. And the second book... well, it's more personal. It's about grief—about losing someone you love and how to cope with that."

Rex looked at her with a mix of admiration and concern. "That's a big topic, but I think it's important. You've been through so much, Sophia. Writing about it might help other kids who are going through the same thing."

Sophia nodded, feeling a swell of excitement in her chest. "Exactly. I want to create something that not only entertains but also helps children understand their feelings. I'm really excited about it, Rex. For the first time in a long time, I feel like I have a purpose here."

Rex moved closer, placing his hands gently on her shoulders. "I'm so proud of you, Sophia. You're turning something difficult into something beautiful. And I'll be here to support you every step of the way."

Sophia smiled up at him, her heart full. "Thank you, Rex. That means more to me than you know. I think... I think this could really work. It's like a new chapter for both of us."

Rex nodded, giving her a reassuring squeeze. "It absolutely is. And I can't wait to see where this new journey takes you. Just promise me one thing."

Sophia tilted her head, curious. "What's that?"

"Promise me you'll still go to Cabo when you need to, but also promise to bring a little bit of Cabo back with you every time," Rex said with a grin.

Sophia laughed, feeling the last of her worries slip away. "Deal. And maybe, just maybe, I'll write a book where Spike and Fifi take a trip to Cabo too."

Rex chuckled. "Now that's a story I'd love to hear."

Epilogue

Beauty twined around their home, their hearts, and their lives. The first anniversary had come with a few battle scars, reifying their undying desire to be huddled up together interminably.

Sophia wore a white dress and held Fifi in one hand, looking around the house as members of her family walked around, conversing, luxuriating in her healthy marriage.

Sophia realized that romantic displays easily undermined the battles outside the façade of these displays.

She remembered the moment she had drank herself to stupor, the moment she was draped over in a cloak of shame, the moment it appeared that the end had finally reared its ugly head. She remembered how easily things could have gone askew if Rex had returned with the temperament with which he left.

Not too long ago, they had been on a knife edge. Their relationship had been precariously balanced, and life had suddenly stopped smiling at them. Hence, it was easy to find another definition of what love truly portrayed.

Sophia reckoned that love was what happened after the shortcomings of a lover became apparent after the butterfly feelings faded away. In her eyes, there was no love that hadn't known endurance and perseverance when it felt easier to quit. There was no love that didn't have nights of bitter tears, days of unquenchable anger, streaks of forlornness.

Sophia remained in a corner, stroking Fifi's back as she remained closeted in her mind. Bianca and Belinda were jumping on a couch.

Adam was spending time with Rex. Sabrina and her fiancé were having an interesting conversation with Jack and Cynthia. David, Jazmin, Roger, and Allen were conversing cheerfully.

There were bottles of champagne on the table. There was a two-layered cake where HAPPY FIRST ANNIVERSARY was boldly inscribed in white letters.

Sophia stood alone, turning the scripts of her love life, reminiscing on a journey where intense loving collided with unexpected compromises. She couldn't think of a better way to make life worthwhile and eventful.

The cheerful faces in the house showed how easily she and Rex had been a great example to their kids. Being able to blend their families without experiencing any real crises was a blessing she couldn't afford to take for granted.

Rex left Adam and walked up to Sophia. He was wearing a white suit, taking up the same neat, almost holy appearance as Sophia.

"We have a beautiful family," he said.

"Yes. I was thinking about the same thing," Sophia responded.

"Adam is a very smart boy. I have a feeling he's going to leave a mark in this world," Rex said, taking a quick look at Adam.

Adam was already standing at Jack's side, taking his hand and listening to the conversation around him.

"We have deserved this, haven't we?" Sophia asked.

"Yeah. We have worked hard for this," Rex replied, kissing her cheek.

Their family and friends congregated around the table and witnessed the cutting of the cake.

The round of applause that followed was loud and cheerful.

"We are already thinking about getting married, Mom? Jeremy and I want to find a convenient date. What do you think?" Sabrina asked after taking Sophia to a quiet corner.

Sophia took Sabrina's hand and led her to the dining table.

"Why have you chosen Jeremy?" Sophia asked.

"He is just different, Mom. He knows how to ask the right question, and he made it clear from the start that he wants to be with me," Sabrina responded and then paused. "But do you think we are moving too fast?"

"There is nothing as fast when the condition is right. You know he loves you, that's fantastic. Now you have to see how kind he can be when he's not happy. I think that's important as well because love will not come through every time. He is not going to be in love with you every day, but if he cares and if he is kind, then you have the best partner you can ever wish for," Sophia concluded.

In the evening, Sophia and Rex spent time together in the living room. They were perched together comfortably holding their drinks.

"It has been a great ride, Babe. But we both know it has been bumpy at times," Rex started, holding his glass forward. "I have always tried to take one day at a time. I think it makes it easier to be as vigilant and loving as possible."

"I couldn't have wished for a better partner," Sophia cut in, interrupting him.

"So, you're ready to have another year-long ride with me?" Rex asked.

"I have no problem at all." Sophia chuckled.

"Even if there are bumps and unexpected obstacles?" Rex asked, staring admiringly at his wife.

"I have no problem at all. I choose you, Rex. I love you, and I'm blessed to have you in my life," Sophia stated, leaving a peck on his cheek.

"Happy anniversary, Babe," Rex said, extending his glass toward hers. As their glasses clinked and their lips parted, accommodating cheerful smiles, Sophia looked straight into his eyes as her face leaned closer and closer to his, settling in a position for a sustained, intense kiss.

THE END

Made in the USA
Columbia, SC
21 March 2025

ce32f5d8-e8b8-4e05-9d36-f1e361f173d4R01